WOLVES AND WHIPPED CREAM

At Hallow's Cove

Ash Raven

100% HUMAN MADE
100% HUMAN MADE
I SUPPORT HUMAN
CREATORS AND MAKERS
NO AI WAS USED IN THE
CREATION OF THIS BOOK

Contents

Hallow's Cove is a charming small town at the juncture of mountain and sea, originally founded nearly a century ago as a refuge for the supernatural. Now occupied primarily by monsters, Hallow's Cove has become a destination for tourists of all kinds who seek to enjoy hiking, skiing, swimming, and more. Visit at any time of year to experience this quaint, old-fashioned town and all the fun activities and natural beauty it has to offer!

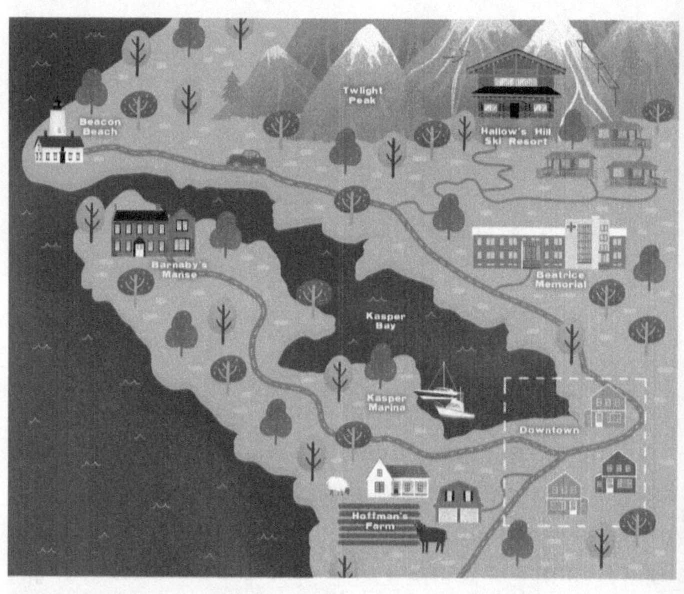

Twlight
Peak
Beacon
Beach
Hallow's Hill
Ski Resort
Barnaby's
Manse
Beatrice
Memorial
Kasper
Bay
Kasper
Marina
Downtown
Hoffman's
Farm

Ice
Rink
Cool Beans
Cafe
Hallow's Cove
School
Town
Hall
Info
Center
Motel
Cafe
Diner
Cove Arts
Centre
Bodega
Rick's
Hardware
Coming Up
Daisies
Bookstore
Thrift
Shop
Gargoyle's
Games
Green
Grocer
Daja
Hairdo

Story Introduction

After a disastrous gallery opening, Roan needs out of London society fast and Hallow's Cove needs someone to fix up the town art centre. It should be a perfect fit, but after a damp reception from the monster residents Roan is worried she'll never outshine her royal lineage, especially when rumours spread she might be more scam than artist.

Clay and Mitch are content with their life in Hallow's Cove, even without an Omega to complete their Wolven pack. Who has time to date when they're trying to keep their business afloat in the off season? But one whiff of the new artist in town, and both Wolven realise she's their fated Omega.

After a few fumbled, flirty conversations and an impromptu poetry night, Clay and Mitch finally share their feelings with Roan, but is she prepared for pack dynamics? And can she convince Hallow's Cove that she's the right woman for the job?

Content Warnings

- Age gap relationship

- Childhood trauma from parents (mentioned)

- Classism and wealth disparity

- External and internal fatphobia

- Scum bag parents

- Ghosting

Chapter One

Roan

I CAN'T TELL IF I'm up, sideways, or in fucking hell when I collect my luggage from the conveyor belt. Twelve hours is too long to sit in economy seating, let alone be trapped in the middle. Between the armrests digging into my hips and the side-eye from the woman who sat next to me every time I took a bite of my sour candies, all my brain power had been spent on minding my own business.

But now I really need it. Stonebridge International is a maze of signs that only leads to a different maze in the car park. I turn down one row of oversized dark cars only to find another. I keep looking for the lift, but I'm only going in circles.

A car horn goes off, and the slow drip of anxiety I've felt about doing this suddenly bursts. A sob catches in my throat and tears dribble down my cheeks. I can't even use my sleeve to wipe them, because my suitcases will roll away. I move across another aisle until I'm on the pavement again, and I can guard my luggage while I calm down.

"Oh, bobble." My mother's condescending voice creeps into my ear as I stand in the small gallery space full of my work. "Your little hobby seems to be... going."

I turn to look at her as my stomach drops into my shoes. No. No, she's not supposed to be here. I specifically requested the gallery be closed tomorrow morning for a private viewing for the Marchioness and her acquaintances. How did she find out tonight is opening night?

"Mum." I try to smile as I look for my agent, but they are nowhere in sight. "What a surprise?"

"Not really. You know Vivian is a trustee, always trying to encourage smaller artists and what they do."

She clasps her hands in front of her stomach, perfectly manicured nails and shining rings glinting in the light. "So when she told me your little friend had submitted your work, I couldn't help myself."

Words catch in my throat at her implication. Since university, I've done whatever I can to pay rent for my accommodations and studio and supplies. I even go by a different name so I don't get the initial advantage that Darrington brings to submissions and applications.

I worked my ass off for months preparing my portfolio and presentation, and then several more months refining my pieces for this show. We thought this was going to be my big break. I thought I was finally out from my mother's thumb. Instead, I was only given a solo show, even for this short run, because of my mother and her title.

"You know," she says, "this would look absolutely lovely at a Mariton. You know Sandra was just saying she stayed at a lovely one in—oh wherever it's called that *they* like to holiday."

I've taken a lot of verbal punches from Lady Angelic Darrington, Marchioness of Farrador, but somehow, this one makes them all pale in comparison. My mother can say what she likes about my hair, my tattoos, my weight even, but insulting my art feels like a cut right to my soul.

All the little parts of me that I bared to the world with each stroke of my paintbrush amount to nothing more than hotel art to her. Some sort of mass-manufactured piece of that she'd sooner turn her nose up at than think about.

My cheeks heat with shame and embarrassment as she compares my work to that of hobbyists and the elderly who need something to keep their minds active. She has no regard for the looks and whispers as she boldly passes judgement on my work, despite the fact she has never once in her life dared to think anything *unbecoming*.

"I suppose it's all well and good that your brother intends to take the peerage rather than you," she sniffs. "But you must settle down, bobble, find a lovely husband who will support you the way I have."

I can't remember most of the night after that. Too many glasses of Prosecco followed by pints at a nearby pub have blurred out the rest of our encounter. I know I'm privileged, a part of the upper crusts of society most people can't even dream of. I've been told my whole life exactly what slim little box I should fit into—how to speak, how to dress, who I should be acquainted with and who I should look down upon.

Everything about what I'm feeling right now, the entitlement and loss, doesn't matter when compared to the rest of the world. A regular being could navigate an airport, and I am a regular fucking human being. I can suck it up and figure this out.

I take a deep breath, grit my teeth, and look for the nearest sign.

"Shuttle to Stonebridge Hellhound Station, floor 5."

The arrow points forward, and after one more confusing sign that leads down instead of up, I catch the shuttle bus that will take me downtown to the coach bus that will drop me off at my final destination. See, I'm navigating and travelling without a security detail or driver just fine. I'm capable of this, just like I'm capable of succeeding without my mother's interference.

I sit quietly in the back of the bus, swiping away notifications from my family while the city fades into the countryside. It's smelly in here, bodies all pressed together. My headphones barely silence the loud children screaming, but they prevent a headache from forming. It occurs to me that I should be hungry this late in the evening, but I'm too shattered to feel anything but exhaustion. I fight to stay awake, reminding myself why I am doing this while I take my lucky handkerchief out of my pocket to stare at the faded red fabric.

The art I produce is meaningful. It captures people's attention and drags them in so they question the meaning of my subject matter. Every painting I create, a little piece of my soul is mixed with the oils and canvas. I can't just give up on all those little parts of me. If I believe in myself, and keep working hard, good things are going to happen for me without my mother's meddling tendencies.

My whole scheme is to prove to her ladyship that I don't need her or her influence. Hallow's Cove is so unlike any of her social circles and so far away from our sphere of influence that there is no string to be pulled or friends to ask for favour. I applied for this artist residency and was accepted by my own merit. I bought my plane ticket with the money I made teaching a painting course for college students.

I will prove to them all my art career is serious, and something I want to do for the rest of my life.

Nobody will know who I am and nobody will look at me differently. This is my chance for my talent to shine unburdened.

Chapter Two

Mitch

THAT IS THE LAST time I stick my dick in honeycomb. You try to do something fun and spontaneous for your partner and you end up with sticky fur from sheath to crease because someone can't control himself around sweets.

Okay, maybe that was the goal. My Alpha mate, Clay, has been in a worse mood than I've seen in a long time. He's a sourpuss most days, but after our last foray into finding the Omega for our little pack, it's been tough to get him to crack even the barest of smiles.

I understand where he's coming from, to some degree. Wolven packs work best with three beings. The Alpha, the Beta, and the Omega. For eons, it was thought that three was a sacred number because that is how the gods destined us to form relationships. Nobody really follows that dark age shit anymore, but that doesn't mean we've evolved out of all our instincts.

As a Beta, my hindbrain is telling me to bury my snout into my Alpha's buttery warm pastry scent and rub myself all over him until he feels better. I want Clay to know we're alright, just the two of us. We have been since before we even moved to Hallow's Cove twenty years ago.

What was supposed to just be a gap year between high school and college had turned into presenting as a mated pair. We'd gone from best friends to lovers over the course of a summer and never looked back. This café happened to be looking for a baker's apprentice as the old troll was ready to retire. Clay had taken the position right away, and I did whatever odd jobs I could find around town until we were ready to buy the lady out.

We've had twenty amazing years together.

But fuck, we're almost forty and still haven't found our Omega. There are matchmaking services, but I think if my mom slips one more of those pamphlets into one of her weekly letters, Clay's going to burn the post office down.

I had always sort of believed that when the time was right, our mate would walk through the doors to our little coffee shop, and I'd do some heroic action move, jumping over the counter and diving nose first into their crotch.

You know, romantic stuff.

Instead, I'm standing in front of our grinder, counting coffee beans and trying not to adjust my junk. We're nearly done for the day, thankfully, meaning I can snag the industrial soap from the kitchen and run upstairs while Clay closes up. A hot shower is calling my name.

Only a few tourists linger around, and a couple of locals too. Since school has started up again, the crowds have dwindled. We get a few DINKs, some retired couples, but already I know we're going to have to tighten our belts until the ski season starts and we can start sending fresh baked pastries to the fancy-pants clientele up there.

The vintage bell over the door jingles as Mayor Louise walks in, speaking loudly with a weird tone of voice that I don't recognise. I'd thought I'd seen all her mimics by now.

"Cool Beans has the best wifi, my lady. You can order anything you need here. And…"

Sweet blueberry jam.

My tail begins to wag uncontrollably as my lips part. Omega. Omega. Omega. My brain loses all function when I smell them.

Our Omega.

Stepping in behind the mayor is a gorgeous, plush human with brown hair and curves that I can just picture sinking my filed claws into. She's definitely an out-of-towner, and the way she holds herself reminds me of the skiers who holiday at the resort.

Elegant, poised, and like she's never had to work a day in her life.

Oh, shit.

As they approach, I reach behind my back and grab my tail. Absolutely not going to show any emotion until I know what type of person she is.

What the fuck was fate thinking? How are we going to live up to any of her expectations? I'm a barista! I know I look nice enough, but I'm not living the high life by any means.

"Mitch, this Lady Rowena Darrington," Louise announces overly loudly. "She's going to help us revitalise the Arts Centre this autumn."

Oh no. Up close, she's even more beautiful. I'm barely paying any attention to what the mayor's babbling on about. I can't pull my focus away from our Omega. She's got white wispy pieces of hair that frame her flushed cheeks, and I think I see tattoos sticking out from under the collar of her shirt and around her wrists. Definitely not what I would have pictured a lady looking like.

"Please, just call me Roan," she insists in a soft, low British accent that makes my tail jerk in my hand. "No need for the titles here."

As she turns, so do I, both of us staring at the town's kinda-sorta-elected figurehead.

"Sure, of course. I won't say anything else," Louise says, making a show of turning her lips into a zipper and closing it.

"Sorry to bother you." Roan turns back to me. "Could I possibly steal some of your WiFi until I can get the dial-up box working at the Arts Centre? I need to order a few things, and—"

"Steal anything you like," I blurt out. My wallet, my pants, my heart. No, wait. I need to slow down. My ears flatten as embarrassment rushes through me. "The password is *Password2*, uppercase P. We had to change it recently."

The mayor gives me a weird look, but I'm not about to tell her I just gave the newcomer my home WiFi password. Roan should at least have access to a line that isn't crowded by half the town. Just because I'm trying not to rush head first into our fated mate's lap, doesn't mean I can't share our nice internet with her.

"I really appreciate it." She smiles and my heart flutters. The smell of blueberries wafts through the air, and I smile back. "What are your hours, just so I know?"

"5:30 a.m. to 2:00 p.m."

"Wow, that's early, right?"

"Yeah, but who can say no to fresh pastries first thing in the morning?" I ask.

"You've got me there." She tucks some of her hair behind her ears, resting her weight on one side so her voluptuous hip catches my attention.

"Oh, we need to head back to the motel. I need to properly introduce you to Connie," Mayor Louise says with mouth still shaped like a zipper.

There's a small dip in Roan's shoulders, but she takes a deep breath, and that same poise from early comes back over her.

"Thank you, Mitch. I'm sure we will be seeing a lot of each other."

Is she trying to flirt with me? My dick is acting like she is, but I honestly can't tell with her accent.

She gives a small wave before she turns to leave, the mayor following right behind her and blocking my view of her round, perfect ass.

Fuck.

Fuck, fuck, fuck.

Chapter Three

Clay

My stomach grumbles as we near the end of the day, but I ignore it, swallowing the little bit of lightheadedness I'm feeling. There's no risk of me dying from skipping a meal or two. Especially when I can still taste cum and honeycomb in the back of my mouth from Mitch's sticky adventure this morning.

I catch a glimpse of my reflection in the stainless steel oven in the kitchen and cringe. What kind of Alpha looks like me? Twenty years spent learning to be my own monster, and baking has turned me more than a little soft. Mitch doesn't seem to mind, but we're nearly forty and not the fit twenty-somethings we used to be. I don't look like the football star I was supposed to be when we first mated. Nor are we able to fuck six ways to Sundays all night long and still open the shop at the crack of dawn anymore.

He's still fit, and just as gorgeous as ever. Even when we were kids, I always remember thinking whoever got Mitch for a mate would be the luckiest Wolven in the world. He's funny, protective, and kind, all wrapped up in beautiful copper brown fur that smells like vanilla, warmth, and a touch of sweet.

If I think about how good my Beta smells for too long, my knot's going to swell and I won't get any of my afternoon prep finished. I need to get it done so I'm not rushed in the morning, which I hate. Maybe I could get him to suck me off while I set up the sourdough to bulk ferment.

As if on cue, Mitch barges into the kitchen, door swinging wildly behind him with a sweet scent that clings to his heated one. With my gloved hands still covered in dough, all I can do is turn to watch him grab the soap by the sink and run out the rear door like the building's on fire.

"Okay, then," I sigh. "Guess I'll close up the front too."

It takes me an extra hour to clean up the front of the café and make sure all our receipts from the day are stored away to take to the accountant at the end of the week. The dizziness has morphed into a throbbing headache, and all I want to do now is fall into bed with my mate and forget that we don't have our Omega or that we're getting older or that money is tight. I lock the back door, then head out the front.

The small flower patch at the front has nearly dropped all its petals. The wolfsbane has a few flowers still clinging to it, but the rest have been cut back. We'll need to get our bulbs soon so they're ready for spring. Another thing to put on my to-do list for the off season. I lock the front entrance and take the other door up to our tiny studio.

Mitch stands in our little kitchenette, his tail wagging so hard that his shorts are struggling to stay up, singing along to whatever music is playing through his earbuds. His fur is still damp in a few places where he couldn't reach it with the hair dryer.

So he stole my degreaser soap after this morning's escapades. Maybe I wasn't as thorough as I could have been when I licked all the honey off his dick. Damn, I could have had a bit more of that sweetness to start my day.

"Hey." He grins as he turns around.

"You ran off quick."

His ears flatten and he gives me a sheepish look. It's not like Mitch to be so quiet. Even after a full day of dealing with customers, he's always chatty. He loves relaying the gossip of the day to me while we make dinner and settle in for the night. The best parts of my day are spent hearing him explain the drama of Hallow's Cove like it's some kind of soap opera.

"Everything okay?" I ask.

"Yeah. I'm just feeling a bit worked up, Alpha."

Alpha.

My cock stirs when he calls me that. Outside of the house, we don't really use designation titles. It's a private, intimate matter for most Wolvens and plays a heavy role in how we live. Some packs ignore the historical and societal hierarchy of our kind. For others, like me and Mitch, we play into it more like we would a BDSM lifestyle. He's my Beta, the glue to a pack relationship and also the catalyst. A Beta instigates relationships with an Omega after the Alpha's approval. His role in our pack is crucial, but more importantly, he's the love of my life. I couldn't imagine being without him.

As the Alpha, my job is to be the one who's got their shit together. Alphas are supposed to be the steady rock in a pack. Right now, I feel anything but strong and dependable.

So while Mitch's words have an effect on me physically and emotionally, I need a different sort of love right now.

"C'mere, Beta." I open my arms and he runs right into them.

We bury our snouts into each other's necks and sigh. Our scents merge and mix like the perfect vanilla cake. He squeezes me, arms struggling to stretch around my thick middle. I try to suck in my gut, but it doesn't stop the doubt that creeps into my thoughts.

"Don't get burnt on me now," he huffs.

"Sorry, sunshine," I whisper, taking another deep breath against the junction of his neck and shoulder.

"Do you want to talk about it, or you still letting it brew?"

He's a good partner. The best anyone could ask for, but I don't have the words to really explain this heaviness settling in me. I press kisses up the side of his neck until I meet his lips. He tastes a bit like blueberries, and I know he's eaten my last experimental cookie.

"Right now, all I want is to share a meal with my mate and fall asleep in his arms."

I'm downstairs by 4:30 the next morning, but I'm more tired than usual. Is this what getting old feels like, or is this further proof I'm not taking care of my mental health? It's probably both, and as Mitch's mother insisted last Christmas, it's probably our lack of Omega to balance us out.

She is the most infuriating Alpha I have ever met, and she won't shut up about us finding our missing pack member. As I knead and beat loaves of sourdough into submission while my croissants are proofing, I keep thinking about those stupid pamphlets.

All those happy, muscle-headed, stereotypical Alphas holding both members of their pack together. It's such an outdated and Alpha-centric view on packs. My parents had that sort of view, and I can tell you right now, that doesn't always lead to a happy home life.

Was I looked after as a kid? Yes. Was my parental pack loving and kind to one another? Fuck no. More than once, I caught my pops begging their Alpha and Omega to calm down and not raise their voice. Or worse, my mama throwing her Alpha and Beta from her nest because she couldn't stand them.

Shouting still makes my hackles rise, and I haven't spoken to them in years. Every once in a while, my sisters will send a holiday card with the whole family on it. My parents are never standing next to each other.

That's why when Mitch and I presented and mated, I was clear that I wasn't going to rush into anything with an Omega or force them into our pack. Whoever they were, the universe would bring them to us when we were ready.

My timer goes off, and I pull trays of pastries out of the oven, firmly shoving any thoughts of my past into a box in the back of my brain. It's a new day, and this batch of pain au chocolat looks perfect. Golden brown on top, all the layers of pastry telling me that it will be light and crispy.

I organise them onto wooden platters with the other sweet pastries, and I take them through to the dark café. There is a soft light from the glass-fronted fridge, but not much else. I put the platters on top of the glass case and flick the lights on, then start arranging today's goodies. Croissants, cinnamon swirls, and pain au chocolat on one side, sunrise muffins and pistachio babka in the middle, and two pies at the end.

At 5:30 on the dot, I unlock the front door. Only a handful of locals come around at this time of morning. Ted, the Bigfoot who owns the diner, always has a coffee while he waits for his daily bun and bread order to be ready. The town Werewolf has started to come by as well. He's a little scarred, a little more quiet than he used to be, according to Lerana, but apparently Jeremy is trying to turn a new leaf after going to some hippie Werewolf retreat in the woods.

Just as I'm about to put on the pot of coffee for the day, someone new stumbles in. The smell of sweet and tangy blueberries hits my nose, and I nearly spill the grounds all over the floor. It's like I can taste sugar-crusted berries with a twist of lemon zest on them without even opening my mouth for a bite. When I turn around, a stunning human is walking right toward me. She takes off her bicycle helmet, revealing a messy pair of braids and I'm struck with the realisation.

She's our Omega.

This short and curvaceous human is ours. The universe has finally sent her our way. While my hindbrain has moved south to my quickly swelling knot, my chest tightens with anxiety. She's a tourist. What if she doesn't want us? Humans don't always have the same connections that us monsters do, and they certainly don't have designations like Wolven do.

Around me, the locals are staring at her like they've just seen a celebrity. What the fuck is that about? I throw a glare at Ted and Jeremy before I make eye contact with my Omega.

"Morning." She smiles at me. "Do you have Darjeeling?"

Heat rushes to my cheeks. I don't have a fucking clue what that is, but she sounds just as sweet as she smells. Her low voice is soft and accented, and not from round here whatsoever.

"No," I grunt, in an effort to stop myself from calling her Omega. Way too forward. I need to control myself. "I can do ya a drip coffee in about five minutes?"

Her smile cracks for a moment, her eyes turning a bit watery, but she nods anyway. She moves to the side, studying my pastries in a way that makes me feel like she's eyeing up a private part of me. There's something almost critical in her gaze, but I focus on getting all the percolators set up for today.

"Could I get a pain au chocolat as well? I was told they're best fresh." The simple French rolls off her tongue with ease. Maybe she's from France. Why would she come all the way out to Hallow's Cove for a vacation, though?

"Sure." I pull out the black tongs and place the pastry onto a plate. "I'll bring the coffee over to you when it's ready."

She smiles again before heading for the oversized armchair by the front door. I set up everything I need for the drip coffee and quickly rush back into the kitchen, so I can breathe neutral air and think of what to do.

Should I tell Mitch? It sounds like the woman who I believe is our Omega interacted with him yesterday. Did he notice it? Her scent clings to my senses until I've not got a single rational thought in my head.

Or did this human not affect him?

My mate hates early mornings, but I'm almost tempted to go upstairs and drag him down here now.

I should just ask if she's staying for a while. That would be good. Plus, if she says that she's leaving this morning, then I won't have to break Mitch's heart by introducing him to our Omega. He won't ever need to know I've met her, either.

I couldn't handle watching my mate get his heart broken if fate isn't on our side.

I grab Ted's tray and head back out to the kitchen. Ted is leaning on the counter now, a conspiratorial look on his face. He hands me his travel mug, but it's only when I hand it back, full of coffee, that he leans in closer to me.

"I heard Louise say that human is bonafide royalty. A marsh or something, I don't know, but the mayor spent all day yesterday giving her a tour and introducing her as Lady Rowena. Lerana said she's staying down at the motel, though. And a bike? Only brings one kinda person to mind, if you know what I mean." He raises those big furry eyebrows at me with implication and then clicks his tongue. "Have a good one, Clay. Tell that lazy sack of bones I said hi."

I swear to gods, Ted and Lerana are just as bad as each other with how they gossip. The universe clearly hasn't paired them together because it would cause a cataclysm. Nobody would be able to survive that gossip mill.

To imply the new person in town is somehow suspicious just because she's staying down at Connie's motel is ridiculous.

Still, it piques my interest even more. I look over at Rowena and see she's staring at us, clearly having overheard Ted. She turns away quickly, shoving her hand into her pocket as he leaves the café.

Is our Omega a grifter? What the fuck would she want with a town like Hallow's Cove? Some of us have money, but even then, we're just a bunch of regular monsters trying to make a living.

My ears droop as I think about that. No. She can't be here just to scam us. I've generally always wanted to believe people have their hearts in the right place. Even if my general enthusiasm for most everything that happens in town is low, I know the people here are good.

Just like our Omega must be.

I pour her coffee into the large cup I usually hide away for myself, and I bring it over to her.

"You need any cream, sugar?"

"Thank you," she murmurs, taking the cup and missing that term of endearment.

"S'not a problem. You in town for a while?" I ask, trying to casually lean against the other armchair to hide my body and my slip-up.

"Until the new year, but maybe longer." She smiles a little, and I wonder if she's trying to be polite or flirty. She takes a sip from my mug, pulling my attention to her mouth. Her lips press into the ceramic, and I wonder what it would feel like to have them press against me. "I accepted the artist residency at the Cove Arts Centre."

Even mentioning the building across the street makes me want to roll my eyes hard enough my corneas detach. That town hall meeting was a damned mess. I was sure someone was going to actually get their throat ripped out this time. While Barnaby has made sure the building's exterior is maintained, nobody has ever bothered to actually put art in there. As far as I can remember, it's never been opened, and nobody can agree on what we should do with the space.

Guess Louise decided for us.

"Aw, well then I guess we're neighbors for a bit." I smirk.

Maybe more than neighbours, if I can get this conversation going in the right direction. I've never really had to flirt a day in my life. All our previous attempts at going out to find an Omega were led by Mitch. He thrives on interaction, and being a bit flirty and naughty in public has always gotten him off. I'm much better at listening, being a soft place to land after a long day at work.

Where Mitch is always keen to follow his impulses in the moment, I prefer to execute a plan that will end in happy endings for everyone. Clearly, this conversation is proving our dynamic works better when we're together and can play off each other's strengths.

She nods. "Yeah, I'm trying to get my bearings and meet people in town."

"Well Cool Beans is the place for any baked goods ya may need, or coffee. When Mitch is awake, he usually makes the fancy drinks."

"And the WiFi," she chuckles. "It's been an adjustment not being as connected as I'm used to. But I'm hoping it brings me some inspiration."

"Where are you from?" I ask, even though I hate beating around the bush like this. I just want to know what her deal is, so we can move past the smalltalk and my poor attempt at chatting her up. "I really like your accent."

"London," she answers. "Are you from town or on a permanent vacation?"

"My mate Mitch and I are from down south, moved here at eighteen and never looked back."

Her face turns red with embarrassment when I refer to Mitch as my mate, and it's only then I remember that it might look like I'm a mated man trying to shoot my shot with a stranger. Even more telling than the small change in her features is the way her scent turns sour like vinegar. Rowena takes another sip of her drink, and I want to kick myself.

Fuck's sake. This is why Mitch leads with the flirting and I follow with reassurance.

"I'll let you get back to work, then." She looks down at her pastry.

"If you need anything, just let me know." I try to force a smile, anything to get her to smell a bit sweet for me again. I open my mouth before I even know what I want to say, but no words come out.

Rowena stands abruptly as I straighten up, her fingers trembling around the cup of hot coffee I just handed her. I'm taken by surprise, but neither of us speak as we stare at each other. My ears tuck back against my head as I get a fresh smell of her sour pheromones. A determined look settles on her face.

"Clay," she says, back straight and her demeanour completely opposite from the person I was just speaking with. "I prefer Roan. You've got the internet. Use it."

She leaves with my favourite coffee mug in hand.

Chapter Four

Roan

I SPILL HALF THE coffee from the mug I just stole down my trousers as I run across the street. That's it. I can't go back to Cool Beans. Fuck, I probably won't be able to show my face to anyone again.

Do they all think I'm some kind of fucking scam artist?

Based on the gossip the large, hairy monster shared with the other Wolven café proprietor, the only way people will be dealing with me is from a distance. Perhaps that's a good thing for now. This will give me a chance to get settled, get stuck in with cleaning up the gallery and show people I'm up for the job I was hired for.

Yesterday was a long day of introductions and reminding Louise over and over again that I was just Roan, a regular person who happened to be an artist. That's supposed to be all that matters about me here. Who my mother is doesn't matter, how I grew up, or anything revolving around class doesn't need to be mentioned. I don't need her getting wind of where I've gone.

The last introduction of the day was with Connie Lumzag, the owner of the retro motel I'm staying at. She is probably the nicest person I've had the pleasure of meeting. Besides being understanding during my sleep-deprived, very late check-in, she also doesn't seem scared to talk to me. When the mayor introduced me again as Lady Rowena again, she didn't miss a single beat when I corrected her. Connie just called me Roan and introduced me to her family.

All the Orcs were excited to talk to me. Her sons were bouncing off the wall, trying to pull me out to their workshop to show me the 1952 Victory motorcycle they are fixing up because it's a British classic. It seems the retro vibes at the motel come from a family of history lovers and vintage enthusiasts.

I'm hopeful that Connie and I will be good friends, even if it's simply for our shared ability to smile and nod while two teenage boys talk a mile a minute about wet clutch plates.

The bike I bought yesterday morning is still stashed in the narrow alley between the diner and the centre. It's a bit rusty, but I need to stick with my budget. Plus, I can't drive, so it's not like I could just purchase a vehicle to get from place to place.

Hallow's Cove is quiet and scenic. It's a little more spread out than I thought it would be, but after taking a map from the Information Centre, I realised there is really only one road I'll need.

The sun is just beginning to illuminate the horizon when I unlock the front door to the Hallow's Cove Arts Centre. During the initial key handover and contract signing, I did my best to keep a neutral expression, but now I let myself feel it all.

Tears well up in my eyes as I look at the absolute rubbish heap I've been put in charge of turning around. Louise told me it needed some cleaning, but this is outrageous. The piles of papers, boxes of decade-old leaflets, and decrepit furniture are all my job to remove, apparently, as is dusting, mopping, repainting, and refitting the whole building.

The building is structurally sound, at least.

My contract includes a small budget for this, but all art supplies and equipment for my projects comes out of my pocket and my meager salary.

Oh, and I've got to have one community event by the end of the year.

I sink into a chair, determined to wallow in self-pity for a few moments before I start being a good person again. The chair gives out from under me in seconds. I tip over backwards, the rest of my coffee splashing across my chest in the process.

My screech echoes in the deserted space as pain radiates through me. The only thing worse is the embarrassment. I know that my weight has nothing to do with why the chair crumbled like a cheap charcoal stick, but my ego is hurt.

Hallow's Cove was supposed to be a new start, away from my mother's unwanted influence, so I could prove myself to be a real artist. But here I am—flattened, drenched in hot coffee, and crying.

Maybe this is a sign.

Rowena Darrington is barely capable of sticking up for herself, and Roan had thought two separate Wolven were flirting with her since arriving. Two Wolven who were mated to each other.

I've known a lot of monsters in my time. Elves, Vampires, and Orcs are all a part of high society circles. University was even more inclusive, but Wolven are still a mystery to me.

Clearly, those two will remain that way, because I can never show my face in that café again.

For several long minutes, I lie on the ground. The broken wood of the chair digs into my light jacket, probably ruining the material. It's only when I'm cold, the teeth-chattering wetness sinking into my shirt, that I finally move.

The bathroom is small and dusty, but there's no trash piled up, and the water runs clear. I clean myself up the best I can, discarding my jacket and top until I'm left in a camisole and hearty, damp trousers.

I've got a list to make.

Sweat pours from me as I drag another box of old papers to the industrial recycling bins at the back of the centre. I want to say that after hours of work, I'm feeling better about my situation, that physical labour has done everything that my mother's housekeeper used to claim it would.

I am, in fact, feeling more hopeless. I've entered some sort of Hydra-possessed building where no matter how much trash I remove, twice as much appears in its place.

Will I ever see the real floors and walls here?

Any other time, I simply would've called in a team of builders to remove all this. A specialist team of interior designers would renovate the ground and first floor gallery, and make the second floor a working studio. Then, as the piece de resistance, I would have instructed my old agent to hire a professional gallerist to man and fill the bottom floors.

But that's not how I'm working anymore. All those contacts? My mother's. I wouldn't know a single bloody person on the European art scene if it weren't for her introduction

I'm a new person here.

Flashing money I didn't earn will only make the rumour mill so much worse. I was hired to do a job, and I can do it. I can't let town gossip or stupid attempts at flirting with mated men get in my way.

When I come back inside, there's a wolf face pressed up against one of the arched windows. I stumble, clutching the base of my throat, until I realise it's the brown Wolven with glasses. When his copper gaze moves to me, his adorable fluffy tail starts to wag as he waves his hand.

I swallow a lot of feelings, but I wipe sweat from my upper lip as I unlock the front door for him. Whatever he's here for, might as well get it over with, since it can't be any more embarrassing than this morning.

"Hey, Roan." He smiles brightly, sharp canine teeth catching the bright sunshine. "Wow this is... a room."

"Hi..." Fuck, what's his name?

"Mitch," he fills in the blank, stretching out his hand. His grip is firm in mine, and when his claws trail across my skin, it sends a zing of arousal right through me. Fuck, no. He's mated and I'm not like that. "I thought I should try to make a better impression."

My stomach drops. Yeah, yeah, makes sense. Tell the stupid human to stay the fuck away, that you're mated. Gods, what the fuck is wrong with me?

"I'm so sorry," I rush out. "I'm not sure what came over me this morning, but that's no excuse. I swear that's not—"

"Oh!" He barks a laugh. "No, no, darlin', he likes 'em flirty. He's just...introverted."

My brows pinch together in confusion even as a thick Southern accent slips through his voice. It sends the butterflies in my stomach into motion, and a blush rises in my cheeks.

"Okay." I nod as my voice trails off. "Is there something I can do for you?"

Chapter Five

Mitch

Marry me.

It's wildly on the tip of my tongue, despite having previously spoken only a few words to Roan. Her jammy sweet blueberry scent is thick in the Art Centre. Sweat glistens across her tattooed torso.

So many tattoos.

As quickly and subtly as I can, I scan her figure. It's a mistake. Whatever sorta bra she has on doesn't do anything to hide her nipples pressing through her shirt. Half my thoughts are on the array of adorable and vintage tattoos that are scattered across her arms and chest, and the other half are focused on her full breasts.

Shit. Fuck.

My cock begins to harden, and I'm worried I'm going to start panting. I need to get out of here. It's bad enough that I can't take my eyes off her tits like a damned pervert, but now we've just been staring at each other in utter silence.

"The mug," she finally says, opening the door wider and letting me step into the centre. "I rinsed it out, let me get it for you."

She drops the handkerchief she's holding on a rickety step stool, turning for a back room. I can't stop myself from taking it, balling it up in the pocket of my hoodie before she comes back with Clay's favourite mug.

"Thank you," I croak, words clawed from my throat like I haven't drunk water in days. I'm so confused about what's happening. I need my Alpha. He always knows how to calm me down. "I better get back to the café."

She nods, politely walking me to the door and locking it behind me. The sound of the deadbolt shoved into place makes my heart hurt a little, but the feeling just tells me more than ever that Roan is our Omega.

With my cock aching, wet shaft pressing into my underwear, I awkwardly waddle across the street and through the coffee shop. It's nearly empty, save for a few older ladies who meet every Tuesday at this time. They've got their tray of coffees and pastries already, so they will be set for at least another fifteen minutes.

"Are you busy?" I rush towards Clay as he stares at his laptop in the kitchen.

"No, what's up?" he asks, nose twitching.

"I have a confession to make, Alpha." My voice turns to a soft whine.

At the use of his designation, my mate perks up. This is serious pack business, and I'm about to lose my mind. I need to tell him, then I need to come.

I set his mug on the counter, empty. I've never brought him this mug without one of my special lattes in it. Now he's going to know something is seriously wrong.

What happened to *let her settle in*, Mitch? What happened to giving her some space before we approached her as a unit?

Clay looks at his cup, and then his eyes go to the floor. Happily, I drop to my knees. Who gives a shit about being sore later when right now, I can shove my face into the perfect crease of my alpha's stomach and crotch? I inhale all the toasted aroma of his scent and whimper.

My hindbrain threatens to override any sense of civility and propriety I have. Roan's sweet scent still lingers in my mind, and now it's mixing with Clay's in perfect harmony.

"C'mon now, Beta," he murmurs, resting his hand between my ears and pressing his hardening cock into my face. "Tell your Alpha."

"I went to make you a coffee like I always do, and I noticed your mug was missing. I thought maybe you left it upstairs, but then when I stepped outside, I saw the new girl hauling boxes across the street.

"And she's not just the new girl. I think she's our Omega. I'm sorry I didn't tell you right away. I was just so fucking surprised, and she's so different than us. But she smells so good Alpha, so perfect."

"I know she's ours already, Beta." He sighs, but it's not with relief. It's like he's sad. "I spoke with her this morning."

My ears perk up and I look at him over the curve of his stomach.

"She heard Ted gossiping, and I didn't make it better like a good Alpha should," he says.

"Is that why she said she'd stay away from us?" I ask, trying to fill in the blank spaces from my conversation with her. "Alpha, we have to fix this. We have to."

I wrap my arms around his leg, which presses my cock into him as well. It's not moments from bursting any more, but I'm shocked it hasn't fully flagged yet. Probably because Clay has agreed she's ours.

We found our Omega. We just need to make her pack now.

"I'm working up a plan, Beta. She's here for a while, and I don't want to rush things."

I nod, my chin rubbing against the bulge of his sheath now. His claws scrape through my fur and I groan as tingles shoot down my spine. When he's like this, it calls out that submissive side of me that turns my thoughts simple. Alpha is working on it. He's got this. He'll make it right.

"What did you take?" he asks suddenly, sniffing the air.

Heat rises in my cheeks and my ears tilt back as I pull out the handkerchief. It smells of dust and sweat, but underneath that it's blueberries, and all our Omega. I hand it to him, and my Alpha presses the fabric to his snout and inhales. A low growl rumbles through him, and thank gods I'm already on my knees, or I would have dropped to the floor.

"You're such a good boy for your Alpha," he groans, unzipping his pants single-handedly in a rush. My tail thumps against the floor as his praise settles over me. "If you wanna be his best boy, though, you better open your mouth."

Clay pulls his pre-lubed cock, red and glistening, through the fly of his boxers. It's long, the tip already leaking just from the scent of our Omega. His knot swells, begging to get buried in a tight hole so he can breed.

I lick the underside of his dick from base to tip, but he holds me in place before I can swallow him. Clay tucks the handkerchief into the waistband of his underwear and looks at me. Drool drips from my jowls as the smell of my mates hits me full force, their two essences combined in one place. Blueberries and freshly baked cake fills my senses until I'm drowning in all its new potential for comfort and debauchery.

"Take out your cock and hump my leg like a good Beta," he instructs without releasing me, a little growl in his command that makes my balls ache with arousal.

We've done similar things throughout our years together. The number of his shoes that I've ruined is a little embarrassing at this point, but gods, does it turn me the fuck on when Clay gets all controlling. As much as he likes his plans and schedules, he's reserved around town.

It's like he saves all this bossy energy just for me.

I spread my knees wider and sit on the top of his shoe. A slow roll of my hips drags my sac across the laces of his canvas slip-on. The scratch of the material teases me while the drag of my sensitive dick on his worn-out jeans makes all my hair stand up.

"Yes, Alpha," I pant, gaze unwavering as I look up at him. "Shit, you make me so hot."

Clay is slow to react to my praise, another thing I've noticed recently. He doesn't smirk like he used to when I comment about how attractive I find him. Once I hit puberty, I knew I was attracted to my Alpha. He's always been the Wolven I wanted as a mate, even before we presented during our second puberty. He is the only monster for me.

Our bodies changing as we've gotten older has never dimmed how much I love his body. His round stomach is just as hot as his flat one from our early twenties.

Clearly, I need to remind him of that.

I kiss the pre-cum from the tip of his dick before I take him down to his knot. My nose presses against the handkerchief and the taste of him coats my tongue. Clay holds my head in place as we begin to rock into each other. His movements are limited as I hump his leg, but every whimper that rises in me vibrates his cock at the back of my mouth.

My claws dig into his ass to push him harder into me. I can't take his knot into my mouth—teeth and all that shit—but fuck, do I wish I could. I want to swallow all of my mate while I bury my snout into the scent of our Omega. The fantasies that form in my head are messy and feral. My hips stutter when I visualise Roan and Clay using me for their pleasure.

"Fuck that's it, Beta," he grunts, rubbing his thumb around my ear. "Take your Alpha's cock."

I moan, swirling my tongue as I meet his gaze. Drool clings to Clay's teeth as he stares at me. Thank fuck I didn't take off my glasses. I need to see this primal side of my mate, to know he's feeling as gone as I am with the smell of our Omega.

My hips begin to stutter, my orgasm building as my body starts to tingle all over. The heavy sensation in my balls draws higher, ready to let out streams of cum. Something flashes in Clay's eyes when he realises how close I am, and he takes the scrap of fabric from his underwear.

"Come on this," he commands.

I want to mourn the loss of her scent, but permission to orgasm is too good to ignore. I blindly reach between my legs and wrap the handkerchief around my cock. Three strokes and all those body tingles spear through my balls. Ropes of cum spurt out of me, taking all my energy with it.

"That's my best boy," Clay moans, moving more urgently in my mouth. He pulls further back and thrusts in harder. He leans into the painful tease of my sharp teeth, grunting each time they scrape across his sensitive dick. "Gimme your cum, Beta."

I hand it over to him carefully. He doesn't hesitate, snatching it from me and shoving it into his mouth. My cum and the sweat of our Omega ruin him. My shaft pulses one weak dribble of fluid out of me as my Alpha tries to taste his whole pack.

We moan together when he erupts in my mouth, hips flexing jerkily as I wrap my hand around his knot to draw every drop of him out. The musky taste of him overwhelms the scent of the blueberries, but it settles my restlessness. A calm washes over me as I swallow every drop of cum.

For a moment, we catch our breath. The ruined handkerchief disappears, probably in Clay's pocket to throw into the dirty washing basket. Our cocks soften and return to their sheaths as we pant from the exertion of a midday quickie. Alpha pets my head, massaging around the base of my ears while my tail slowly wags with pleasure.

One of the ladies back in the café hollers something. I can't make out what, but it brings me back to reality. The café is open, and we are supposed to be working.

"Do you need me to get the tigress balm?" he asks, offering me his hand to help me.

My knees crack as I get back to my feet. Gods, I hate that. "I think I'm alright, Alpha."

Clay looks at me skeptically, and I know in about ten minutes, he's going to wave that jar in my face and tell me to use it. Ever since our last physicals, when I mentioned more pain in my joints, he's been vigilant about making adjustments for me. Right now, though, all I need is a little more of a snuggle.

"We found her," I whisper, wrapping my arms around his neck while he pulls me in tighter. "Our Omega."

"Yeah," he agrees. "But we can't rush her. She's got to come to us, to want us. I think we need to give her a bit of time to settle into town, and then we approach her."

"However you want to do this, Alpha, we'll make her ours."

Chapter Six

Roan

IN AN EFFORT TO avoid Cool Beans for as long as I can possibly manage, I buy the cheapest selection of tea I can handle from Mother Earth's Green Grocer. It's not loose leaf like I prefer, or even Darjeeling for that matter, but the lovely older Minotaur lady who runs the shop told me it was the best they had. She tries to make a fuss, and I have to promise her that if I don't like the kind I bought, I'll return it.

Every cuppa I've had this week has been bitter and without any milk, because I don't have a fridge in my little room. Connie's design choices are spot on when it comes to mixing patterns and colours, but they're lacking a bit with extra amenities. It's a room, it's safe, and it works for now. The Lumzags are super helpful and lovely, but I think it's because I'm the only person staying at the motel right now.

Actually, all of town feels a bit ghostlike at the moment.

Despite being here for a week, I'm still waking up at an ungodly hour, and I commit the greatest sin on the planet. I microwave my morning tea. It lacks all the goodness of a proper cup, but I force it down because my funds are limited until I can get the centre up and running as intended.

The trash is now gone from the ground and first floor. Instead of finishing the second floor and seeing what's up in that old workspace, I've decided to move ahead with patching and painting the gallery spaces. Even though I don't get cell service here, my phone is still good for taking pictures.

With everything documented and a list of potential supplies and questions, I have a date with the hardware store...once it opens. Considering it's still dark outside when I cycle into town at 5:30 in the morning, I need to fill my time with something.

I sit on the floor of the gallery and sketch, slowly filling pages with ideas for events to hold at the Art Centre, evening classes, and portraits.

So many new faces, new people.

Since the first charity dinner my mother and father had dragged us to as children, I've been obsessed with portraiture. The old manor house was filled to the brim with family paintings, beings of all shapes and sizes, and I'd stared at them the entire night. How their eyes could be empty or overflowing with emotion. How subtle features were suddenly centre stage with a simple stroke.

It's been my passion since my art GCSEs, capturing someone's expression in my mind's eye and creating a version of them that is familiar and strange all at once. During uni, I tried venturing into new mediums, but I always come back to my beginning. A clean sheet of sketch paper and pencil.

Recently, though, only two faces have drawn my eye. They're growing more obscure and abstract as the days roll on. While I'm building up a muscle memory of how to sketch their forms, I've lost the intrigue. The angle of Mitch's glasses aren't right, and the greys on Clay's muzzle seem to be taking him over now.

Their eyes are missing something, too.

After a while, my stomach growls, and I make the bold choice to venture to Ted's Diner for the first time since I heard the giant man gossip about me.

"Hi, honey, what can I get you?" a faun asks before she's even set down the giant menu in front of me. "We gotta special on for our Bigfoot platter, and there's a fresh blueberry pie this morning if you're feeling something sweet."

It's on the tip of my tongue to say *always*, but I ask for a hot, unsweetened tea with milk. She gives me an odd look at my request, but scurries off. I scan the menu for the cheapest item that isn't oatmeal, but my eyes wander over to the glass-front fridge. Between the steel containers and jugs of milk, one crisp, dark pie sits untouched.

"Here you go." The waitress sets down a mug and a separate, full glass of milk. "Saw you eyeing up the pie. Trust me, Clay makes the best desserts in town."

A fluttering sensation starts in my chest at the mention that Clay, a mated monster, has made it.

"I think I'll have a slice," I say, hoping my cheeks don't give away what's happening to the rest of my body.

"You want whipped cream with that?"

"Oh, yes please." I grin.

She smiles for real at my answer, her freckles practically glowing with cheer. I painstakingly use a paper straw to transfer millilitres of milk into my tea until it becomes the correct shade of beige. The diner has a few patrons, and I do my best not to overtly stare at any of them for too long.

A generous slice of pie with an intricate crust design is placed before me, a perfect squirt of cream decorating the top. I leave it for a moment, opting to pull out my sketchbook again while my tea cools for a few minutes. After a few extra, non-Wolven portraits are rough-scratched into my book, I turn my attention to the pie.

I'm not Mary Berry, but my fucking gods. Everything about this is perfect. It's sweet and tangy and buttery and crisp. The flavours burst on my tongue and I want to live in them forever. I slump back in my booth and moan softly.

Wow.

I think I just had an orgasm.

I scarf down the rest of the pie like a greedy little animal between slurps of weak tea. It's only when I'm swiping a finger through the indigo syrup left of the plate that I feel something like guilt for devouring it. It doesn't bother me that it's pudding; it's the fact that Clay made it that sets my inside rolling.

He didn't make this for me, obviously, but my brain is doing some Olympic-level gymnastics to make my enjoyment feel like I've hurt someone. I haven't. There is nothing wrong with a person enjoying a slice of pie. It can be my little treat, a guilty pleasure to enjoy as I progress on the Art Centre.

Nothing more.

Rick's Hardware Store is oddly familiar and comforting. It reminds me of traditional English hardware stores, narrow aisles and crowded shelves stacked high up to the ceiling. The large, tan Minotaur behind the counter smiles when I walk in, and I hope that means he's remembering our introduction rather than any gossip he's heard about me.

"Morning, Roan." He smiles.

"Hey, you alright?" I ask.

His heavy brows scrunch up. "Yeah, why wouldn't I be?"

"Sorry," I say quickly, nervously tucking a strand of hair behind my ear. "Sorry, I just meant *how are you* in a casual greeting sense, nothing serious."

"Ooh," he draws the syllable out. "Well I'm alive and a pretty lady's just walked in, so I can't complain. What can I do for you?"

I pull my sketchbook out of my backpack and begin explaining the vision to Rick. I show him the photos I took of the gallery and explain different concerns I've got, and he nods along politely. I don't even realise how close he's gotten until his fingers brush against mine suddenly. His hot, minty breath fans across my cheek, and I blush.

A deep growl behind us makes me weak in the knees.

Chapter Seven

Clay

THE FIRST HARD FROST is coming soon. If I didn't have the extra tension in my shoulder telling me we have a cold snap coming, Mitch's boundless enthusiasm would be all the alert I need.

It's time to buy spring flower bulbs from Rick's.

The café has a decent-sized planter built into the yellow stucco fronting that Mitch and I have carefully cultivated to nurture the bee population in town. We grow gorgeous blooms of marigolds, wolfsbane, lavender, hyacinth, bluebells, and violets. Every spring, it overflows with stunning blues and purples that pop off the yellow of the café.

Mitch saw the weather report first thing this morning and couldn't wait to tell me. His excitement was contagious, and I promised him I'd go to Rick's as soon as he opened up. I can't wait to get my hands dirty digging through the soil. For me, planting bulbs is like watching a well-laid plan come to fruition. It gives me a sense of pride that I need.

We'd gotten a little swamped with a birding group, so I'm walking over thirty minutes later than I intended.

The sun is shining, but the air is much cooler than it was last week. Fall is setting in quicker than it did last year, and I'm excited about it. There are gorgeous hiking trails around Hallow's Cove, and both of us prefer the crisp mountain air over the humid stuffy summers we get.

Across the street, the Art Centre is empty. Maybe Roan's sleep schedule has leveled out, so she hasn't started her day yet. I hope she's getting enough rest. Mitch has been covertly watching her clear out all the junk for the past week. It's probably misplaced, but I'm proud of her for doing all this work by herself. I only know what a brief internet search could tell me about her, but our Omega's fucking brilliant.

Fuck knows why she's here and not showing at fancy galleries like she had been. I even saw that one of her paintings sold for ten thousand pounds. If that's not famous, I don't know what is. I showed Mitch while we were watching reruns of *Mated in Manhattan* in bed last night, and his eyes had sparkled with excitement.

The Bookstore is closed as expected when I cross the road, and the shop next to it has been boarded up for a little while now. It's not a good look for there to be empty shops on Main Street. It was bad enough that the Art Centre was empty and one of the last buildings before you headed up the mountain. But right dead centre in town?

Not good for business.

Maybe Rick will buy it up and expand his hardware store. He's young and ambitious. He's good friends with Barnaby, and I like him well enough when I see him. With the hours I work, I don't deal with a lot of people the way other shop owners do. Mitch has been the face of Cool Beans since we took over, and that's for the better.

A bell chimes overhead when I walk through the door, and I'm immediately hit with the scent of blueberries. Roan's low voice carries softly through the store as she laughs at something. My heart stutters, and when I see Rick leaning over her, his hand brushing against her wrist, I see red.

My lips pull back, the hair underneath my sweatshirt rises, and a growl rises up inside me like it never has before. It rips through their soft conversation and makes them both look at me. For a second too long, Rick's hand doesn't move away from my Omega.

I step forward with every primal intention of just biting his fucking head off. I inhale sharply, and that tangy blueberry scent filling the air has gone all syrupy sweet. Roan looks at me with wide, hungry eyes for a moment, before pressing her lips firmly together.

"Sorry, sorry. I'll come back another time," she apologises, running down a different aisle.

As the chime over the door innocently jingles, I blink. The clouded, feral feeling in my chest swirls down to my stomach like rotten milk.

"Dude, what the fuck?" Rick says incredulously, leaning against his counter.

He's a big guy, taller than me, but I imagine we're close in weight. Definitely a more age-appropriate partner for Roan. But fuck me. She is our Omega. Ours. He shouldn't be making a move on our mate.

"Why were you flirting with her?" I counter instead of just speaking plainly. "She's here for a job."

He snorts, "We're all adults here, Clay. I think she can have a bit of fun too."

"Not with you," I growl again, pointing a finger at him.

He stands up taller, squaring up against me, and all those Alpha traits I keep locked down start bubbling up. My fists curl up and I bare my teeth, ready to fight someone I almost consider a friend. But he was touching my Omega. She doesn't need anyone else except the pack she has at home, ready to wait on her hand and foot.

Rick huffs, his nostrils flaring. I could take him. I might not win, but I wouldn't lose either. We'd both end up bruised and stupid-looking and...

"Shit." I back up, even if my instincts are telling me otherwise. "Shit, fuck, I'm sorry. I'm being real fucking outta line."

"No shit, Sherlock. What the fuck is going on with you?"

I drag my hands across my face and smooth back my ears. Gods fucking damn it. Should I tell Rick? There isn't any other white lie coming to my mind right now, but I can't have the whole damn town gossiping about us. Roan hasn't even come back to the shop since that first morning. We've just been watching her like a pair of creeps.

"Cat got your tongue, Clay?" Rick taunts, posture still up and ready to fight me.

There is no part of me afraid of a fight. I know what it feels like to get hit by a Minotaur, barreling down the field at full tilt just because you're holding a ball. But I am not that kind of Alpha. I'm not ruled by the toxic ideas my parental pack tried to teach me. There is nothing wrong with being open about my feelings. I can trust Rick.

"No. I just got territorial when I came in, and that was wrong to you and her. I'm real sorry, Rick. It was uncalled for."

He crosses his arms, and I wouldn't blame him for not accepting my apology.

"She's not an object. She can flirt and do whoever she wants."

"I know, I know." I swallow the lump in my throat. I've got to actually say the words so we can put this to bed. "Mitch and I believe Roan is our fated mate, to complete our pack."

There's a beat of silence. Rick's hard features soften into something tired, and maybe a little sad. It doesn't last before he plasters on a look that's more exasperated.

"Tsk, 'course she is. Of course. You know, there isn't a human in town who hasn't been fated to someone. I don't get it."

"We don't really get it either," I offer. "But I know for Wolven, we can smell it."

"Yeah, yeah, I smelled how fucking hot she got for your strong guy bullshit." He waves a hand at me and walks back behind the counter.

"Humans are different, and confusing."

"That's what makes them fun." He smirks. "Now what can I do for you?"

With supplies bulging out of my tote bag and Roan's abandoned sketchbook in my hand, I head back to the café. The street is busier now that it's lunchtime, and I have to awkwardly weave through people. I hate crowds. I hate feeling like I'm being rushed down the sidewalk by other people. I just want to be back in my kitchen where I belong.

I drop my bag near the welcome mat and customer coat rack, clutching our Omega's book to my chest like it's a prized possession. A part of me desperately wants to look inside, but I don't want to overstep or invade her privacy. Is her sketchbook like my box of recipe cards? Secrets meant only for those who are worthy?

Mitch hands a customer a large latte with a foam coffee bean design on the top as I round the counter. He looks at me for a moment before following right behind me into the kitchen. I'm in a fucking trance as I stand on the other side of my large steel table.

"Whatchya got there, big guy?" he asks.

"I growled at Rick," I murmur, before launching into a full rundown of what happened this morning. He listens, taking his glasses off when I try to explain how feral I felt, and how worried I am about what that means for our potential pack.

"You aren't the Alpha that raised you," he says. "And it sounds like our little Omega didn't mind the show."

"Does that make it worse? That she wants a kind of mate I'm not?" I frown, staring at her sketchbook at our table. The smell of graphite and blueberries wafts from it, reminding me of the first sunny day after a long winter.

"Maybe we should move up our plan." Mitch wraps his paw around mine and kisses my cheek. "The first step to forever is just right across the street."

"Let's finish out the day, and go speak to her then."

Chapter Eight

Roan

I TRIED REALLY HARD. I swear on my grandmother's sapphires that I fought every fibre of my being to not touch myself. I'm trying to be a good person here.

But I'm only human.

I don't know what came over me after Clay's weird outburst. Because it was definitely weird and not hot as hell. I certainly didn't run back to the gallery in a wave of horny humiliation.

I tried scrubbing the first floor on my hands and knees, physical labour and all that. But I crumbled like a biscuit dunked in tea. Discarding my wet brush and leaning against the wall by the small open balcony, I push my jumpsuit down to my calves with my boots still on.

I open my knees and run my hand across the curve of my stomach, over my mons. My panties are damp with sweat and arousal as I press down on my clit.

Clay's voice echoes through my thoughts as I rub myself. His paws are so big. The pads look soft, though, like they would grab my ass or tits with gentle possession. He always smells so good. I could bury my face in his neck while he buried himself in my cunt.

While my forearms begin to cramp a little, I get more desperate. I want to come. I need to come to get this out of my system and go back to ignoring my crushes.

Because it's not just Clay filling my sketchbook—it's his mate, Mitch too. His brown fur shining copper under the sunshine. His tail wagging with excitement while his sharp teeth sink into me.

Would they fuck me together? I've seen porn. I've known plenty of horny artists. Not all monsters are monogamous, and some don't even have mates, just like humans don't. *Threesome* is probably my second most common spank bank reel.

Just the idea of being in a Clay and Mitch sandwich makes me moan. My hand moves faster. The material is soaked, and I don't think I've ever been so aroused in my life. I pant, rubbing my clit harder and faster, my body jiggling with my force. I'm so close, so close.

"Please," I murmur under my breath. "Fuck."

I press my head back against the wall and close my eyes. Christ, why does the vision of them fucking me have to be so hot? Their fur brushing against my skin as they use my body for pleasure. My fingers move faster and harder against my panties until I can't take it anymore. My hips jerk up as I orgasm, pussy clamping down around nothing while I keep stroking my clit until my body is begging me to stop.

My eyes squeeze shut as I come down, ragged, panting breaths echoing around the empty room. Nobody is going to know what I've done, and yet guilt settles in my stomach all the same. I reach for my lucky handkerchief like I have done for a week, but just like it has been, my back pocket is empty. I never lost it before, but every day I can't find it, my anxiety grows.

When I started university, I took a course with an older American artist who believed anyone could be anything. She humbled me more than anyone else at that school. She taught me the value of simplicity and seeing the world through my mind's eye, not just the squishy marbles in my head.

When I graduated, she gave me that handkerchief to remind me to keep all my eyes open and believe in myself.

Right now, I feel sightless and lost.

I scrub my eyes with my clean hand and roll over onto my knees so I can stretch my back before I get dressed. These floors aren't going to clean themselves.

The bright afternoon sun warms the air. Subtle mirage lines appear as I stare up at the tall, flaking walls of the ground floor. The hard wood is clean, and I think with a bit more scrubbing and a good wax, it will be in perfect condition. I'll need to replace a few boards upstairs, but I can do that tomorrow. Right now, I could really use a cuppa and quiet place to sit again. Maybe Ted's does takeaway and I can check out the Bookstore.

When I cycled to the Info Centre on Monday, Naia mentioned speaking to Barnaby Hallow about my plans for this centre. I know that America doesn't have the same sort of classism that it used to, but I didn't expect to have to break out that old training in a town like Hallow's Cove. If Barnaby's family has owned this town for a long time, he will probably have a lot of opinions about what he wants to see displayed. Surely, he's on whatever committee the mayor said selected my portfolio for this job.

I go to the toilet and splash cold water on my face and neck to get rid of the sweat and dust before I head off on a different mission for today. Ted's doesn't do a takeaway for hot drinks, but Lerana was more than accommodating, handing me a hot ceramic mug with a wink. I promise to bring it back before I go home for the night.

Before I leave, I look back over my shoulder, and a different patron is staring at me with a flush to their pale green skin. There's no subtle way to sniff myself, and I'm terrified it's not sweat that some of the monsters in town must be smelling on me. My panties are dry, it can't be that. I refuse to believe they can still smell my cum after a few hours.

A small chime announces my presence in the Bookstore.

"No open drinks," a woman behind the counter with a laptop open says without looking up.

I stand on the small welcome mat for a moment, wondering what I should do. This is a fresh cup, it's too hot to just chug it down. The steam wafts up against my cheeks even as I try to take small sips to get some of my money's worth.

"I can watch it if you wanna browse," the woman offers. "You're Roan, right? I think I missed ya when Louise did her tour."

"Yes, thank you." I smile and walk carefully up to the counter. She folds an old envelope up into a square and sets it by her closed laptop. "Do you know Barnaby?"

"I'd like to think so." She smiles, little sharp points of her fangs showing. Ah, so she's a Vampire. "What can I do for you?"

"I was told to speak with Barnaby about my plans for the centre. I'm just wondering if you could tell me a bit about him before I have to face him."

She makes a face and snorts. "Do what you want, it's your space now. If he gets a bug up his craw about it, I'll set him straight. He's a crotchety old man sometimes."

"Maisie" — a voice comes from the back of the shop — "you wound me with your harsh words."

A tall, dark-haired man in a suit walks towards us. Maisie rolls her eyes and smiles at Barnaby. He was curt during our introduction, but now he seems almost playful when he speaks. He's dressed more professionally than either of us, but when he steps behind the counter, he kisses Maisie on the head before dropping his jacket on the back of her stool.

"It's good to see you again, Roan. I've mentioned to Maisie a few times that it'd be good to have you around at the Manse." He smiles, a quick flash of his fangs. Is he teasing me? It's not uncommon for Vampires in high society to be cheeky bastards, but I did not peg Barnaby as that type based on our first meeting. "Or at the very least, around the back to look through our storage. I've collected so much art over the centuries, it would be nice to have it safely displayed."

Oh my gods. He's not just some grandson of a grandson. This doesn't change much, but it could easily mean he has museum-quality art he wants cared for. It also means that when we were introduced, he would have understood the exact magnitude of my family name.

"Oh yeah, then we can replace that boring landscape in the foyer with that nude painting of you." Maisie smirks. "Really welcome people in with this newfound friendliness."

"I may not be one of those French girls from that godsawful film you made me sit through, but at least my modesty is covered." He blushes and folds his arms disapprovingly.

A smile creeps up my lips, and the apprehension in my shoulders slowly fades away. "I'm sure people in town would love to see you with the Leo treatment, Barnaby. Really helps us get to know the founder."

Maisie laughs, and a small bubble of hope forms in my chest, I feel like I'm making another connection in town. There's a small circle of people I'm forming, first Connie

Lumzag and now Maisie. There and then, I decide I'm going to do my damnedest to befriend her.

"I've got the ground and first floor cleared out, and I plan to make them a gallery space. If you do have anything you want displayed, just say the word," I explain. "Naia mentioned I should come down here to approve my plans for the space?"

"She was just trying to scare you. She's a bit growly with most people, and I'm surprised you ran into her at all." Barnaby waves his hand.

"It's your space," Maisie insists. "We're all just excited to watch you work."

"Since it appears you'll be here for a good long while, might as well do it to your standards now, rather than wanting to change it again in a few years."

My eyebrows scrunch up a little at the way he says that. Shouldn't I design the space in a way that best suits the town and future residency artists? My plans aren't overly ambitious, but they leave space for the Centre to grow and for the town to use it as a multi-functional space.

"True, plus the town council is full of overly opinionated people who can never agree on anything. Don't let them throw off your groove."

"They approved my application, so I guess a majority of them like me, right?" I chuckle sarcastically.

"No, Louise went behind all our backs and set up this whole thing without anyone else knowing." Barnaby rolls his eyes. "You'll get used to her *go get 'em* attitude eventually."

"Oh." I blink, trying once again to school my features. Maybe this explains the origins of the rumours. Nobody really picked me. Hell, I don't even know how the mayor decided on my portfolio. Did she choose me just because a quick search of my name results in a myriad of annoying articles about my family? Was I not chosen on merit? Did I take this position from someone more deserving?

"We should get a coffee or something when you've got an afternoon free," Maisie says. "Gods, I can't even drink anymore, and I'm jealous of all that free coffee they must let you have."

"Yeah, let's put something in the diary," I agree, not really listening. "Nice to meet you, Maisie."

I carefully take my mug of hot tea and walk back to the Cove Art Centre. The tall, tan sandstone building feels more like a spectre of my past when I look at it now. The neoclassical facade reminds me more of home than it has any right too, like the ghostly, polished fingers of my mother's hands are wrapping themselves around the building, clawing away any hope of proving myself capable. Where I had pictured a beautiful array of flowers flowing down from the Juliette balcony in the warmer months and seasonal lights wrapped around the columns, now I just see the grim and barren face of a residency I didn't deserve.

Chapter Nine

Mitch

I FEEL LIKE ONE of those little toy cars that have been pulled back, and I'm just waiting to shoot off. There is so much energy zooming through my muscles and I can't stop wagging my fucking tail. Am I sweating too much? Should I shower before we go over there? I don't want to smell bad. Our Omega needs to know what I really smell like and not what my nervous sweats reek of. At least I should brush my teeth. And maybe put on a nicer shirt.

Roan must have dated a lot of impressive people before she came to Hallow's Cove. I can only imagine the type of people she's used to being around. It's definitely not the sort of good time we're used to, bottom shelf rosé and some candy from the discount bin at Mother Earth's. We are really going to have to make an effort to show her we're better than any sophisticated royal fancy pants. There isn't anything I'd change about our life, it's been twenty years of amazing love and friendship and intimacy. I just want our Omega to feel as good as I do, no matter what we're doing.

I wipe down the pastry cabinet and take the trash out of the bin to haul outside before we leave. I rush through the sparkling clean kitchen with determination. Finally, the last chore of the day. Done.

"Let's go go go," I say, trying to scooch my Alpha away from the sink so I can wash my hands. "Lock the back door, and then we can leave."

"Beta," he warns gently, voice stern, "take a deep breath."

I do as I'm told, inhaling that deep buttery delicious scent of his. It goes right to my head, which I'm sure is not the intention for this exercise. I'm moments from running across the street and tackling Roan, not simply asking her out. I wasn't ever the football star like Clay was, but I could be now, I think.

We take a deep breath together, and Clay rubs his hand up and down my back until I'm done washing up.

"I know you're ready," he says. "But we gotta be patient for a little longer, and we are only asking her to dinner. She could say no."

My ears droop, and I frown at him for being so practical against all the positivity I'm pumping out. In my heart, I know he's trying to save me from a major letdown. He's guarding his own heart too after how badly last time went. As much as we want this, and as much as I just want to jump right past all those traditional dating standards and move Roan into our very tiny studio apartment, I'm smart enough to know it's not a good idea. For one, where would her stuff go? That studio is barely big enough for one of us, let alone a whole pack.

"And she could say yes," I remind him, just because I can. "Hope never hurts."

"You're right." He smiles a little, but I can hear the doubt he's trying to keep a tight lid on.

We turn off the lights and walk out the front door.

Roan stands across the street, staring up at the Art Centre. She's got a mug from Ted's in one hand, but no bag this time. Clay has her sketchbook tucked under one arm and his hand in mine as we jaywalk to stand next to our mate. A huge gust of wind blows her dark hair over her shoulder, and I'm hit right in the face with her jammy sweet scent mixed with a tinge of musk.

My head cocks to the side as I inhale that deep scent under her natural one. My eyes flutter closed for a brief moment when my cock twitches like it knows that smell better than I do. Is that her cum I'm smelling?

Oh, fuck.

Clay said she was excited by his Alpha attitude, but enough to touch herself? The vision of Roan's delicate fingers covered in arousal goes right to my cock and knot. Our Alpha got a little territorial and she got horny enough to masturbate. Was she thinking about him? I hope she was, because honestly, looking at Clay now, I want to jerk off while thinking about him too. His thick grey fur, his soft stomach, his pecs, that serious look he wears most of the time.

Gods.

Fuck, focus on the task at hand.

"Heya, Roan," Clay calls out, raising her sketchbook in the air.

Her eyes are red-rimmed with tears threatening to fall when she turns around. We step up quickly, looking up and down the street. A few families linger on the street after school pickup, but it's otherwise deserted.

"You okay?" I ask.

"Of course." She forces a smile. "Just—excited about the progress for the centre. What can I do for you?"

She looks between the two of us nervously. I don't miss how she puts a bit of space between us. Is she scared of us? Did I come on too strong, or is it because I stole her handkerchief? We washed it, but I've been keeping it on me as a little token. Even though it doesn't smell like her anymore, it makes me feel close to our Omega.

"You forgot this," Clay says, handing over the book. She looks a little confused, like she didn't realise she'd even left it behind at Rick's. She carefully takes it from him, clutching it to her chest, a look of hesitant relief coming over her as her shoulders relax. His hand lingers in the air before falling back to his side. "But we wanted to talk to you about something."

The colour drains from her face, and I can see her metaphorical defence line take up position around her. Her shoulders become stiff and the mug in her hand starts to tremble. Oh, no. This is not good. Not good. The red lights are flashing so fast in my head.

"It's about something fun." I grin, lies forming in my head just seconds before the words start spewing out of my mouth. "We're having a poetry night next week, and we wondered if you'd like to display a couple paintings and maybe do a little talk between poems?"

"Oh, uh, are you sure?" she asks, fingers curling around her sketchbook even tighter.

"Absolutely," I say in a rush. "You're a part of the community now, and we want to hang out with you."

Hang out? *Hang out?* What the fuck is wrong with me? That's not romantic. That doesn't say *we want to fuck you six ways to Sunday and then eat breakfast in bed together.* A hangout implies platonic feelings, which I most certainly do not have.

Her eyes flick to Clay, and I'm not sure what I'm more worried about now, her saying no or my Alpha's expressionless face. Even Gabe down at the game store has more emotion during the day than my mate right now. Clay hates surprises, hates last-minute plans, and I've just decided to put together a whole event without asking him. I nudge him a little, and he blinks.

"We could use a bit of culture 'round here," he agrees carefully, his words very measured.

"I—yeah, I can do that. Next Tuesday?"

"Yep." I nod. "We can help carry anything you need across the road."

"Okay, I'll see you then."

"Just give us a holler," Clay says, hand squeezing mine in a silent message that he is really, really not thrilled with my idea.

She nods and walks back inside the Arts Centre.

Clay is going to kill me.

The café is surprisingly crowded, buzzing with excitement for a new activity in town. Who knew so many people in Hallow's Cove would be interested in poetry? I know there are few hippy-dippy people in town, but it feels like everyone has crammed themselves into our modest shop. Our regular coffee klatch group is front and centre, and Barnaby and his new mate Maisie are also here. In fact, there are quite a few of the nocturnal monsters in town here, when I can't recall the last time I saw them. Maybe we should do more evening activities. One of the teachers from the night school has already asked me if this will be a regular thing.

The fact that I'm still steaming milk proves Clay did not kill me. I did have to brush up on my word art skills to make the posters I plastered around town in a wild sprint. My mate is standing next to one of the large paintings Roan brought over this afternoon. The oils are still wet, so nobody can get too close, and Clay is more than happy to play bodyguard while our Omega goes around speaking to people handing out small little postcards about the two paintings. I can't believe she painted two new pieces for us.

I figured she'd have had some mailed here to at least start the gallery, and to tide her over while she works on new things, but maybe not. I don't know why she wouldn't want to bring some of her old art here, but maybe it's an artist thing. New place, new paintings.

She claims they are still "raw," more in progress than finished, but I can't stop staring at them. One is of the matriarch of the Lumzag Clan, her forest green skin painted amongst a sea of vintage patterns that are still sketches. Apparently, they'll become the different fabrics around the motel to express her love for the retro aesthetic. The gold bands on her tusks look almost real and touchable on the canvas. Her eyes sparkle with mirth, even if the grey streaks in her black mullet are prominent at her temples. Connie is here in the crowd somewhere, but I can't see her from behind the counter. I hope she loves our Omega's work as much as I do.

The second painting doesn't have a face yet. The figure is masculine, the torso slightly fuzzy around the edges, but that's all. The sketch of the head shape doesn't reveal any defining features. Are they supposed to be a human? A monster? Someone else from town or someone from her past? Maybe the card explains it, but I'm hoping I get to ask her myself. The background of this painting is the opposite of Connie's. There are fine details around the edges, lines and shapes that look like little blobs from where I'm standing now look, but when I helped her set up the makeshift easels, I saw that they were tiny words.

Influence. Hobby. Talent. Juvenile.

Clay looks at his watch, then whistles loudly. The room hushes, even if that noise always makes my ears ring. He stands awkwardly in the small space we've made for the brave souls willing to participate in our thrown-together poetry night.

"Thank y'all for coming out tonight. Mitch and I really appreciate the support for our first evening event. We just ask that you're polite to everyone who comes up here tonight, and that you have a good time."

He nods to the first person who signed up, and lo and behold, it's Connie. There is a cheer that I'd expect at a ball game rather than an artsy night like this, but I'll take it. Enthusiasm is good. As Connie begins, I watch Roan squeeze around people until she's standing next to me. I give her a smile, trying to be fun and positive even as I see the nerves on her face. We listen to Connie's poem about motherhood and finding herself anew. Roan claps the loudest once she's done, and it does something to me, making me all warm inside seeing her form connections with people in town.

"We've been workshopping that," she whispers to me. "I'm so happy she wanted to share tonight."

"It was really good," I agree. "Do you want to share a slice of pie?"

Her eyes go wide, and I pull out the slice of blueberry pie I've been saving all afternoon. What can I say? We've all been on a real kick for blueberries recently. I squirt two swirls of whipped cream on top while the next poet steps up. Jeremy anxiously looks in Barnaby's direction as he starts speaking.

I focus on my Omega, watching her spoon break through the buttery crust and gooey blueberry filling. She makes sure to get a decent amount of cream on her bite before she brings it to her lips. Maybe I'm staring too much. It's probably too much, but I'm more turned on than I thought I'd ever be watching someone else eat my Alpha's baking. It helps that she's ours, but seeing her lips stain purple with it has my cock hard.

Her eyes flutter closed and she nods as she chews. I take my own bite, my mind swirling around the idea of licking whipped cream off my Alpha's cum-covered cock. Something to consider in the future as a way to torture Clay, once Roan is truly ours. I hope she's got a bratty streak like me. I think it would be good for our Alpha, to keep him outta that grouchy mindset.

Jeremy ends his poem to an uncertain round of applause, but I think he looks pleased as he steps back for Clay to bring a stool to the centre of the stage.

"If Roan is ready, we can have a quick talk about her work before we finish out the night with a few more poems."

Her eyes go wide for a moment before scarfing down one last bite. She scurries up in front of the crowd, and a change comes over her. A seriousness settles over her features while she sits down.

"Thank you, Clay and Mitch, for having me," she starts. "I realise some rumours have been flying around about my position here, so I can't express how grateful I am to be given the opportunity to discuss my work and dreams for the Cove Arts Centre.

"As Mayor Louise has introduced me to most everyone in town, my given name is Rowena Darrington, but my preferred name is simply Roan. I attended the Royal College of Art in London for both my bachelor and master's degree in fine art. The two portraits behind me are examples of the style I have been developing for well over a decade now, and one that I hope will keep evolving as I grow as an artist and a person."

Clay makes eye contact with me like we're in some sort of spy movie, nodding as if he's confirming this information. This is similar to what we were able to find when we looked her up online.

"Does anyone have any questions?" Roan asks.

One of the new humans in town lifts his arm. "Are you going to paint everyone in town?"

"Only with their express consent. I like to spend time with each person as I start work on a new piece, so being able to have some rapport is important."

"Why'd you come all the way out here?" Rick asks.

"There are very few places in the world like Hallow's Cove," she begins. "When I saw the application for this residency appear, it felt like fate telling me to leap into something out of my comfort zone."

My ears perk up a little when she mentions fate. That feels like a good sign.

"On your little card, it says you were inspired to paint Connie because of her aura," Jeremy says, and I see several people in the room slouch, an air of exasperation settling over us all. Here we go. "How are you able to see this? Are you attuned to nature somehow, or is there a practice you follow?"

Roan blinks several times while she processes how to answer him. He does one stint in the woods to better himself, and he's gone down the druid pipeline.

"In this context, aura is a metaphor I use to add a level of mysticism to why I'd like to stare at the gorgeous Connie for several hours," Roan jokes, garnering a few chuckles and *hell yeah* from Connie's mate, Gnurl. "I believe to paint someone's portrait, you must understand them. You're preserving a piece of their soul on canvas, and you should do them justice."

More questions pop up about her work and plans for the Arts Centre. She answers each of them with a measured amount of enthusiasm and sincerity. Our Omega knows how to speak in front of a crowd. Each question answered seems to relax her and the crowd more, another connection being laid between us all as a community.

"Will you be hosting any classes?" Maisie asks as a final question.

"I would like to once the space is functional, but I can't give a firm date on any potential class yet."

Clay steps up to the platform, holding out his arm for her to take as she hops down from the stool. He whispers something in her ear that has a red tinge rising on her cheeks. She walks back towards me, smelling sweet, and I just want to pull her into my arms.

I settle for a smile, a low five, and a night of weird and wonderful poetry from the residents of Hallow's Cove.

Chapter Ten

Clay

THE GENTLEMAN IN ME is screaming as he watches Roan wipe down another table. She is not only a guest, but our Omega. We should be working while she enjoys a cup of tea and another slice of pie or cake. She certainly shouldn't be helping us close up shop.

But I can't say I hate it. Seeing the sleepy side of her, yawning and rubbing her eyes, is adorable, and it makes me want to bundle her up and drag her to our bed for a good snuggle.

My own yawn punctuates that thought. I'm dreading my alarm clock in the morning. As successful as this impromptu poetry night was, I am not planning a repeat any time soon. Mitch stacks up the last plate to be run through the dishwasher and ties off the compost bag filled with coffee grounds.

"You did great tonight," I say to Roan again. "I can't wait to see whatever else you create."

"Thank you." She smiles. "I think tonight was a smashing success for you as well. The poems were surprisingly good."

"Don't lie," Mitch calls out. "Flora's poem made no sense."

"It rhymed at least," she says. "And it's not about critique, we're just here to facilitate a sense of trust and free expression."

"So diplomatic," Mitch groans, leaning over the coffee bar.

I give him a look, one that I hope conveys steering the conversation back to our original plan of asking Roan out on a date. Even after the bumbling invitation last week, she's been firmly avoiding us. Tonight is the first real time we've had with her.

"Had you met a pack of Wolven before coming to town?" I ask, trying as ever to play it cool.

"None that comes to mind. Leonids, Shifters, Orcs, and Vampires, sure." She shrugs a little. "I get the impression city life isn't for most monsters."

She's not wrong. A lot of our kind don't fit into the cramped spaces of human-built cities. There are a few around the world where monsters can travel with ease, but they've never really appealed to either of us. When we used to talk about taking a vacation, it was always to somewhere even more remote than this, somewhere we didn't have to see anyone else, do any customer service, or wear clothes.

Would we move for our Omega?

"Is city life for you?" Mitch asks.

Roan pauses, fingers rubbing over the microfibre cloth she's holding. "I don't know," she answers after a short while. "I grew up, went to school, worked, all within a few kilometres of each other. I could walk to the shops or cycle down to my agent's office."

"Not so different than us, then," he jokes. "It's what makes Hallow's Cove so nice. Even as we get more and more tourists, we keep things small and easy."

"There are a few hole-in-the-walls around town." I edge a bit closer to her, and Mitch does the same. "We'd be happy to take you out to 'em sometime?"

The look we get is confused, to say the least. Roan's cheeks are tinged pink and her eyes are wide. What is she thinking? Is she embarrassed to be asked out by me? By us?

"Um—"

"Like a date with us, Roan, not like friends or casual or whatever." Mitch's rushed explanation rises with the spike of burnt vanilla in his scent. She looks a little relieved by his words, but her blush has spread to her ears. She blinks a few times, like she's trying to figure out how serious we are, and I wish I could read minds so I could ease whatever thoughts are running through her head. "Only if you want, but we'd really like to take you out."

"Can I answer you tomorrow?" she asks, her soft voice barely a whisper.

"'Course, sugar," I say, taking a step back. "Do you need a ride home or anything?"

"No, Maisie offered to drive me already."

We've already agreed to take the painting back to the Art Centre tomorrow, so Roan simply throws her backpack over her shoulder and waves as we watch her walk outside and turn towards the Bookstore.

Is it murder if I kill Ted for being loud and annoying right as I open the shop, or would I be doing a public service to the town? If he points one more furry finger at the portrait of Connie, I'm not liable for where this coffee pot lands.

"I'm just saying, Clay, that ain't what she looks like. She's got... stuff," he says, waving his hands like he knows anything about art. The painting looks exactly like the Orc.

"Connie seemed more than pleased with it last night," I grumble, taking another sip of my coffee. My nose wrinkles. I'm missing my Beta's special touch. This cup is bitter and not the sweetness I'm craving this morning. "Which you'd know if you'd been here for the poetry reading."

"Look, some of us have bills to pay and customers to serve." He rolls his eyes.

"Don't be a dick, Ted," Jeremy grunts.

"You'd know all about that, kid," he taunts back.

"Would y'all just shut your pie holes?" I demand, eyes burning as I try once again to rub the sleep away from them.

Mitch and I spent most of the evening too anxious to sleep. Our Omega's reaction to being asked out was unsettling. And while I wasn't expecting her to jump for joy right into our bed, I was sorta expecting a bit more of an answer. If we'd asked last week as planned, I'm not sure we'd have gotten a yes, but at least we wouldn't be waiting.

While I can keep my feelings quieter, letting the resignation to her rejection settle in my gut, Mitch isn't taking the waiting well. He has always been much more optimistic and hopeful. Not knowing is eating him up. I had to practically pin him to the mattress last night just to get him in bed. He had so much nervous energy, threatening to wear holes in our floorboards with his pacing.

The timer by the kitchen door goes off, and I head back to pull a few trays of buns and croissants out of the oven. The flaky, buttery crusts are beautiful, perfect with years of practice. This sort of order usually keeps my mind settled, but now the pastries just seem boring. They are missing a zing that I can't deny I'm craving.

Just as I pull a fresh punnet of blueberries out of the fridge, Mitch stumbles in through the back door. He's got my old high school hoodie on and a pair of slippers on instead of his shoes. His copper fur sticks out in odd places, but with the way he's still running his paws over his face, it's not going to be styled any time soon, either. His glasses are askew, their arms not secure around his ears, but resting just underneath.

I take off my gloves and pull my sleepy Beta into me. He smells like the sweetness I'm needing this morning, and I don't miss the way his tail lazily wags when we share our scents. I hook his glasses up and around his ears where they're supposed to be. He kisses me softly, if not a little sadly. There's no resisting the need I feel for another hug, to feel my mate in my arms as the chance to have this with our other mate hangs in the balance.

"Deep breaths, sunshine," I whisper. "Do you want to pull up a seat while I get Ted's order ready?"

"Yes, Alpha."

Mitch shuffles out to grab one of the stools we keep tucked behind the coffee counter, only to come running back in like the building's on fire. He rips the fresh pair of gloves from my paws and throws them away.

"Hey!"

"She's here," he says, tugging hard on my hands.

The defeat that I resigned myself to twists into knots in my gut. I swallow, trying to stop bile from rising into my throat. We walk back out into the café, and there she stands next to the small display fridge, staring at the bottles of juice and overnight oats. The bluish lights illuminate the dark circles under her eyes, telling me none of us got the sleep we really need.

Despite my own exhaustion, those Alpha instincts rise up from my hindbrain, and I'm speaking before I mean to.

"You should still be in bed, sugar," I chastise Roan. "Did you cycle here?"

"I couldn't sleep," she murmurs, a sheen of sweat across her temples.

"Do you want to talk somewhere private?" Mitch asks, side-eyeing Ted, who couldn't look more obvious about snooping if he was carrying a microphone.

"Do you?" she asks quickly, her chest rising as she breathes a bit heavily.

"No," I say, sensing the apprehension in her voice.

I'm not sure what it's about, but whatever her answer is, the two patrons at the café aren't going to bother us. This is it. We waited, and I'd wait a month of Sundays for our Omega, but I need to lay out our plan for her. We've done this all backwards, because even with Mitch's impulsiveness, I can't stop myself from joining him when it comes to asking our mate out.

The knots in my stomach twist tighter, and I have to fight to get the words out. "We'd like to officially start courting you, to join our pack, Roan. Can we take you out to dinner?"

Just like last night, her eyes go big, but her lips part with shock. She looks between us, a strange, fresh note in her scent as she adjusts her backpack. Nerves crawl up my spine like annoying bugs, and Mitch isn't doing much better next to me. His tail is stiff and tucked against his back leg.

She takes a final look from me to Mitch. "You both want to date me?"

"We want to do more than date you, darlin', but we can start there," Mitch assures her with a flirty wink that makes her blush.

"It's how Wolven packs work. Three is sort of our magic number."

She sets a hand on the counter, and exhales a huge sigh of relief. Followed by a nervous chuckle, and then a giggle so bright that it makes my world feel at peace. Mitch's tail starts to wag, thumping against mine.

"So is this a yes?" Mitch asks.

"Yes, I'd very much like to be courted, or whatever." She grins, the curl of her lips calling to me. Elation is a heady feeling. One little success on our long plan to get Roan to stay with us forever, and I'm ready to scoop her up and taste her right here on the counter. "I don't suppose you'd have a cuppa now, though?"

"Yeah, I can have a coffee." Mitch eagerly jumps behind the espresso machine and turns it on to start building up pressure. "Have a seat on one of the couches, and I'll bring 'em over for us."

She doesn't move right away, her eyes snagging on me. My fingers itch with the need to pull her softness into me. I want to feel her against me, warm and comforting, for just a moment, to let go of all of the stress and nerves that had built up while we waited, but I can feel Ted burning holes into my back. Instead, I settle for a little hand-holding. I wrap her small fingers between mine and let my hindbrain have this one little pleasure.

I kiss the back of her hand, breathing in the sweet smell of blueberries.

"Y'all go get cosy," I explain. "I've got some work to do."

A little pout pulls at her bottom lip, and already I know I'm in trouble. I want to take hold of her again, but I want to bite and suck on that pouty lip too while my knot is stretching her pussy out as she comes over and over again. "Better put that away before I give ya something—"

Mitch coughs loudly before I say something I shouldn't, but that doesn't change the fact it turns Roan on. Her blueberry scent is thick and heavy with need. It's going to be a special kind of torture for our Beta to have to sit there politely while she smells like dessert. I can't tear my eyes off hers, and the tired and hungry look in them that calls to the feral side of me.

"How much milk, Roan?" Mitch asks, setting a steaming mug of tea next to his coffee.

Chapter Eleven

Roan

After running away from the café last night and over to the Bookstore, I word-vomited everything to Maisie and Barnaby. They're the only two in town I'd consider personal friends and confidants. The Lumzags are wonderful, but I'm too embarrassed to ask Connie if a hole-in-the-wall is what I think it is. Beyond just being physically older than me, she seems to know everything. I don't want to look silly or like a perv by asking her about glory holes in Hallow's Cove.

Maisie is the one who talked me off the cliff of despair. The guilt I felt for flirting with them, the worry about cause a rift in their relationship, all the fear I'd had built up in my head over nothing had resulted in one long crying session into her cold, vampiric shoulder as her husband stood there awkwardly, waiting to hand me tissues to blow my nose.

"Wolven are a very traditional and ritualistic species," Barnaby had instructed me, stacking book after book onto the desk in the back room of the shop. "Less secretive now, but they don't advertise their whole way of life like some. I can assure you they form triads or packs, rather than a pair like many monsters."

I nodded, unbelievably tired and relieved all at once, like the anxiety of being a potential homewrecker had finally stopped chasing me and I was getting my first easy breath. A lot of the titles presented were self-help books, and I tried not to take that personally.

"Sounds hot," Maisie agreed. "Mitch's always been super nice to me when I've been to the café. He just lets me sit and smell the goodness."

"And Clay is a good being. Honestly, the only reason we don't socialize more is because he works those odd baker's hours. He and I have gotten into many heated discussions during town hall meetings." Barnaby nods, holding up a bin for me to throw away the used tissues I'm clinging to.

"Look, my unqualified advice, as someone who did the whole miscommunication trope," she says. "Be up front with these guys. If they are serious, they'll like you as you are."

Maisie had been right.

Mitch's warm hand on mine makes all the anxiety seem stupid now as we sit on the worn couch by the window, watching the sunrise. Some of the knots in my chest loosen as I look at him in the warm light streaming through. His fur glows, his oversized hoodie and adorable slippers making him look more like a soft toy I want to cuddle all day. He takes a slow, appreciative sip of his coffee and I do the same to my tea.

Darjeeling.

"Is it right?" he asks, a nervous flick of his ears.

"I can't believe you found any in town," I say, breathing in the almost spicy, floral scent.

"Clay ordered it special. He's a big softie like that."

"And what about you?" My fingers tease the short fur around his paws, sliding through downy hairs.

"Aw well, ya know, I'm just the hard, silent type. Big strong monster man." He grins, teeth all on display as he jokes.

Heat rises in my cheeks as a saucy question pops into my head, but I take a sip of my tea instead. He doesn't need to know I'm thinking about his hard cock now. It's only when Mitch's nose twitches that I realise he can smell something more than just coffee and my deodorant.

"What are you thinking about?" he whispers, leaning in a little closer.

The sunlight catches on his fur, a burning slash of red through soft brown, and I'm in awe at how beautiful he is. He shifts, pulling his knee up to the couch so we're facing one another. My heart flutters even as I lean into him.

"I'm thinking about you."

"Thinking about me how?" he pushes, waiting for me to admit that I'm horny.

I don't know what's gotten into me recently. Something about this town has turned me into a sex-hungry animal.

Every night I've been here has been spent with my fingers stroking my clit until I'm ruining another pair of panties to the thought of Mitch and Clay fucking me. It's a miracle that laundry at the motel doesn't cost me an arm and leg.

"Seems like a pretty heated thought, with how much you're blushing," he whispers.

"If only you knew," I say, trying to play coy like I was raised, like how everyone else I've known has flirted.

"Tell me." The intensity of his gaze is there and honest, but none of the teasing.

There is only one other person in the café now, and he's sitting in the far corner drinking his third cup of coffee. Still I lower my voice, leaning so close to Mitch that our noses nearly touch. While I'm more tempted than ever to tell him I'm thinking about his hard dick, I'm closer to kissing him. I want to feel his soft lips on mine. Will his short fur tickle? There's only one way to find out. I just need to lean in closer.

"Did you know Wolvens can smell their mates? That's how they form packs," he blurts out. "Most beings sorta smell the same, but mates smell different."

I pull back just an inch. "What do I smell like?"

"Blueberries." He smiles, his warm breath fanning across my neck and making me shiver. He breathes in deeply, cold nose ghosting over my skin. "But there is something more under it that's thick and syrupy."

I shift in my seat as arousal seeps into my panties. My stomach roll catches on my leg when I push up on Mitch's thigh to smell him the way he has me. He smells warm, homely. Good and comforting and delicious. A rhythmic thump sounds behind him when I linger, trying to breathe him in and figure out what he smells like to me so I can surround myself in it all the time.

"Roan." He clears his throat with a nervous little laugh.

I sit back down and realise I might have stepped over some unknown boundary. Mitch pulls a pillow over his lap, but I don't miss the bulge in his loose sweatpants. He doesn't look away from me, even as my cheeks heat uncontrollably.

"Clay says I smell like vanilla and sunshine," he offers.

"He's right," I agree, because suddenly that's one of my favourite smells, one I want to wake up to every morning and fall asleep next to.

I sit full back, giving him some space if he needs it, and honestly, because I need it too. My body is hot, blood pounding through me faster than it has in a long while. Seeing Mitch react to me turns me on. That could be addictive.

"I don't think if I say what I was thinking earlier would help either of us right now," I tell him, even if I still want to flirt.

"Save it for later then." He sighs, a little dramatic.

A giggle comes out of me that sounds so obnoxious, I cover my mouth. "Sorry, sorry." I take a deep breath.

"Why?" he asks, cocking his head to the side. "S'cute when you laugh. Like a little hyena."

My mouth drops open in shock, and he barks with laughter until he snorts, which in turn makes me laugh again. It's contagious and stupid, but I feel more relaxed than I have in a very long while.

In the few days leading up to our first date, I spend a lot of time staring out the windows of the Art Centre at the coffee shop. The yellow stucco walls are fading in some places. The flower bed out front has had small gardening work done to it. The dark soil looks freshly turned and there are tiny signs placed around it.

And for all my daydreams and staring, they have both been leaving messages for me in the upstairs window. They're goofy and hard to read, but when I'm taking a break from cleaning the top floor of the centre, they always make me feel giddy with anticipation. When I'm getting too into my head, I look out the window and smile at whatever doodle one of them has done.

Today's message comes with a suggestion. "Wear your boots" is scrawled in thick marker with blue tape holding it to the window. Around it is a series of Post-It notes that make a heart. I'm not sure I know what that means for our date tonight, but I'm excited. It's not like I was planning on wearing my rubber clogs like I am now, but Clay taking the lead like this is doing something for me.

I shove one final bag of rubbish out of the back door, heaving it up and over the railing, and let it fall into the giant bin. I noticed Ted moving the industrial bins closer to my building and took that as a sign that he didn't really think I was a scam artist anymore.

The final space of the Cove Arts Centre was described to me as a studio when I accepted the role. Mayor Louise and I had many conversations about what I'd be walking into, because neither of us really knew what state it would be in. It wasn't exactly the easiest to walk through for her to take pictures, but she assured me it was safe enough. She had the original floor plans scanned and emailed over to me after I signed.

The second floor looks more like a loft than a workspace now. There is a kitchenette that was fitted sometime in the sixties, before the centre was boarded up. The bathroom is full vintage, down to the tiles. Immediately, I snap a few pictures to show to Connie. She's going to love this. Maybe she and the boys would be interested in repurposing this stuff for their rooms, or maybe she'll know if it's worth anything. The bathroom downstairs, while still old, doesn't have this feel, this sense of life.

I wipe my brow with the sleeve of my ratty university t-shirt, making a note in my sketchbook. This could be good to use for a portrait background series—how we as individuals bring life into dead spaces, but that life can linger even after we're gone.

On the cycle home, I forget about my ideas for work. My belly churns with nervous energy, a long list of things I need to do before I'm ready for my date with Clay and Mitch. I couldn't ask Connie about glory holes around town, but I did tell her I had a date tonight. She'd already known, because Ted told Lerana, who told Gwen at the game shop, who told Mrs. Harrison at the inn, who told some guy named Jake who has a shop that does something, who told Rick, who told her.

It's a long, winding game of telephone that had ended with Connie and her adult daughter Bula barging into my room asking me if I had agreed to elope with Mitch because Clay was dying. I damn near fell off my bed laughing before getting them straightened out. In the end, I'd promised to give them a little fashion show before the guys came to pick me up.

"Where are you going again?" Bula asks, picking over the minimal jewellery I brought with me.

"I don't know. They've been keeping it a secret." I have to shout from the bathroom as I flick another layer of mascara on.

"Where could it possibly be that we don't know about?" Connie huffs, seated on my closed toilet lid. "You've got Ted's, and there's that strip mall by the highway that's got pizza, Chinese, and tacos."

I try not to make a face. It shouldn't matter where this first date is, because it's the thought that counts. They want to take me out, and that should be enough. Nothing wrong with tacos and a drive. Maybe they want to go stargazing or something. I saw a pamphlet for that when I got a town map, I think.

"Oh," Bula coos. "Maybe they want to cook for you?"

Now that does sound like a dream. I could use a real meal, one that isn't from a microwave cup or haphazardly pressed with an iron. But why would I need to wear boots for that? Oh fuck, what if they want to take me on a hike? I'm not one of those outdoorsy girlies. I like the inside.

"I'm trying to keep an open mind," I say. "I'm not the most experienced with dating."

"How old are you again?" Connie asks.

"Twenty-six, but I think I've gone on like three whole dates in my life that weren't arranged by my mother."

Those I had been on were plenty. For about a whole year while I was at university, my mother had me on a monthly rotation of men and monsters of good breeding who she deemed worthy of being tied to our family. I finally put a stop to it when one of the human men tried to force himself on me after I told him I wouldn't be going on a second date.

It's a miracle I escaped from her watchful eye at all, now that I think about it. But then again, I've been dodging every phone call, email, and text message she and my brother have sent me.

A walkie-talkie goes off, and Connie practically jumps out of her skin. "Why the fuck are you using those?" she asks Bula.

"Because they're fun, Mama. How else were Jazz and Rilly going to tell us the boys have pulled up?" she squeals with delight.

Sweat breaks out under my armpits, and I start running around to put on any final touches. Boots, extra perfume, the earrings Bula picked out.

"Is this okay?" I ask in a panic, showing them the outfit I've had on for almost thirty minutes. "I don't look gross?"

"You look great, hun. Knock 'em dead." Connie smiles, her tusks teasing the corner of her cheeks.

Bula hands me a small clutch that she's lending me for the evening. "I put extra condoms in there," she whispers. "Don't do anything I wouldn't do."

Chapter Twelve

Mitch

"Damn," Clay murmurs next me as we stare at our Omega walking down the stairs in an absolutely sinful dress. Roan looks like she poured herself into the tight-fitted black number that hits the top of her thick thighs.

"Should we have dressed up more?" I ask, looking down at our nice jeans and buttoned-up flannels. Clay sucks in his stomach as my gaze moves over him, and I want to say something, but he hasn't been in the mood to listen to my praise.

As she approaches, I get a better look at her dress. The low neckline shows the full curve of her breasts, highlighted with body glitter. Every step she takes towards us hypnotises me with a shiny jiggle of tits. Shit, I'm gonna look like the most love-drunk idiot all night, staring at my two mates.

Unlike Roan's boots, I had the pleasure of digging up our Luraitta cowboy boots and giving them a good shine.

Anytime Clay puts on his boots, it just takes me right back to being eighteen and figuring out how we wanted to work. We did the traditional courting for a few months, and every night we'd end up with our boots knocking together, unable to control ourselves.

I can already smell the heady blueberry scent coming off our Omega as she looks at us. Her cheeks are flush, hopefully with excitement, and her dark hair is all piled up at the back of her head except for the bleached bits that frame her face.

"You both look very lovely," she says with a big grin. "I didn't overdo it, did I?"

"No, no, not at all," I say in a rush. "You...you...you look—"

"Gorgeous, sugar," Clay fills in for me as the words get trapped on my tongue. His tail wags against mine, excited for a night out at last.

His plan is unfolding right at our feet, and if things go as they're supposed to, we will finally have the third member of our pack, our Omega, a creative and kind human who I would have never expected to be interested in us. Hell, she's a damn royal, but looks like a natural climbing up into the middle seat of our truck.

She tucks her legs between the gear shift and we both squeeze in next to her. I throw my arm around her shoulder to make room, and give Clay a steadying squeeze. He looks at me over her head, and I think I see real hope in his light eyes. As we pull off into the setting sun, all our knees rocking together as we head towards the dance hall, I feel like I'm getting a glimpse of the future.

"So where are we going tonight?" Roan asks over the quiet radio. She sounds a little nervous, and the instinct to comfort her warms my chest.

"It's a place Clay and I used to go to a lot when we were younger. It's always a hoot." I lean over a little to knock into her. I'm not sure if we're at the hugging stage yet. I want to. Oh, how I want to pull Roan onto my lap and just let our Alpha drive on forever, just the three of us making the truck smell like blueberry pies and hot afternoons laying in the sun.

"A hoot?" she giggles.

"Yeah, it's what us old folks call a good time," Clay says, trying to maintain his usual serious demeanor. It fails as the corners of his lip twitch up when he glances over at us.

"Please, you are not old."

"Says the lady twelve years younger than us."

"He's got you there, sugar." Clay smirks.

"I am perfectly aware that I'm younger, just like I was perfectly aware of it when I first flirted with two older Wolven because I thought they were hot."

"Uh-huh, is that what you call all the times you ran away from conversation?" I ask.

Her cheeks burst with glowing red embarrassment. Calling her out might have taken this in an awkward direction, but I'm curious.

"Maybe I like the chase?" she counters.

"Or," Clays pushes, turning the truck down a gravel road.

"Perhaps I was caught up in my thoughts and didn't want to flirt with married men?"

"Didn't you wonder why both of us were flirting back?" I twirl a bit of Clay's fur around my claw as I lean into Roan. Her warm body calls to me like flowers to a bee. I want to drink her in, taste her while our Alpha watches.

"Not for a second," she shrugs.

"Well, we can practise some more once we're inside," Clay announces as we roll to a stop.

The dance hall is more of a warehouse about thirty minutes outside of town, and it's the best place to go for line dancing. Not exactly a well-known spot, as far as we can tell from our years of coming out here. Tourists don't bother swinging by.

In the early years of us having full control of the café, Darlene's Disco had been a reprieve from always having to be customer-forward. Here, we could be messy twenty-somethings who would happily fuck in the bathroom and tell off any rude dickhead.

I'm not sure you could pay me to sit my bare ass on those counter tops now. But the memories are vivid, and Darlene still lets us in, despite what wild kids we were.

The bouncer raises his bushy eyebrows at Roan's passport, but hands it back with a nod for us to pay the cover charge. Clay drops the cash in the bucket, then we get our hands stamped, and we're finally inside.

Twanging, fast-paced music plays overhead just as a band starts setting up. People mingle around every corner, all of us gussied up for a night out.

"What're ya having, sugar?" Clay calls out to Roan over the music.

She pulls him down by his shoulder so she doesn't have to shout. "Pint of a lager."

He nods, already knowing what I'm drinking, so he makes his way through the crowd to the bar. He's already said he wasn't drinking tonight, but that he wants us to have fun. Another night, we'll organise a different ride home so it feels less like Roan and I are being chaperoned.

"Not what you were expecting?" I ask, following her gaze around the bar. Not much has changed since the last time we were here. It's still a cavernous space big enough to hold Giants, if they want to line dance.

"Honestly, I'm not sure what I thought would happen tonight," she says over the noise. "Maybe dinner. But is there anywhere in town that isn't Ted's?"

"There's one place in town that's pretty nice, but we promised to show you a hole-in-the-wall." Her cheeks heat up when I say that, a flush that heads right down to her sparkly breasts. "What?"

"I—"

"What's what?" Clay asks, putting two glasses down on the table we're standing around. He looks from me to her and back again.

"When you said hole-in-the-wall, I didn't think you meant this," she says.

Clay's ears drop a little at her admission. This date was his idea, something a bit different and fun to show Roan what we're like outside of work.

"What'dya think we meant?" I press, determined to keep my optimism until it kills me.

"Glory holes." Roan snatches her pint and takes a large gulp before either of us can react.

Clay cracks first, his lips spreading into a wide grin before he laughs in full force. His belly shakes, and I can hardly keep the tears from slipping down my own cheeks as I laugh, too. Holy shit. Our Omega thought we'd take her to a glory hole for a first date?

"And you agreed to come along anyway?" Clay asks, leaning into her.

Oh, that little slip has loosened him up already. Smug contentment settles over me. My Alpha likes to think he can suppress all his natural instincts, but they are there. He just needs to trust himself to let them out.

"Well, yeah." She crosses her arms, pushing her breasts up. "Either I was going to get a show, or be mistaken."

"A show?"

Oh, now that is an idea. Generally, exhibition and voyeurism aren't my thing. Clay and I are both private people with our sexual affections. But putting on a show for our Omega? That sounds hot as hell. Would she just want to watch me service our Alpha? Could she resist while I'm swallowing his cock? Does she want to see what it's like to be fucked by a monster with a knot?

"If you're wanting a show, sugar, the only actors involved will be us," Clay promises, tucking hair behind her reddening ears.

I take a drink of my hard seltzer, the bubbles making my mouth tingle just as the band hollers on the mic that it's time to get dancing. The crowd rushes into lines, and we pull Roan towards the back where we can teach her the steps. She doesn't exactly get it, her turns are a little awkward and her boot-stomping a bit early, but she's smiling.

At one point, they play a slower song, and I let Roan and Clay have a moment. They make slow squares, two-stepping near the edge where I'm watching our half-finished drinks. My chest constricts as I watch them get lost in each other. Clay's features are softer, his grumpy expression melting into an almost smile while Roan looks up at him. She has one hand on his neck, her fingers brushing over his fur in a way that I can only imagine is driving him wild. I love my Alpha, and seeing him accept our Omega fills a part of me I didn't realise was empty.

Once the song comes to end, though, Roan is just as quick to drag me in for more dancing. She laughs as she tries to keep up with the steps. We keep encouraging her, and her confidence grows, even if she's still off-beat. Maybe it's just another excuse for us to come back, so we can have another lesson in dancing.

Her grin stretches from ear to ear as we shimmy through a few songs. Sweat beads around her temple as we finish our drinks and head for more at the bar.

Before Clay can even suggest some water, Roan's already ordering it and three Diet Cokes for all of us. A giddy sort of pleasure zips through me when she takes charge, but I know it's going to ruffle Clay's feathers.

Which he needs. He needs to get out of this box he's stuffed himself into. He can't show our Omega what he's like as an Alpha if he's not honest with himself.

"You can get the next round." Roan smiles as we head for the table. "That's how I've always done it."

"Sugar." Clay's voice is rumbling deep when he looks at her. "You aren't buying a damn thing again tonight."

"You don't—"

"No, we do need to," I cut her off. "It's how dating works for us. Let us handle it."

"Oh," she gasps. "I'm sorry, I didn't mean to be insensitive."

"We know," Clay says. "That's what courting's for, so we can get to know one another."

"So tell me about you," she insists, lips sealing around her paper straw.

"Well, let's start with the fact that I landed the hottest football player in our hometown," I start, ready to spill all the silly stories I have about Clay. This is my element. I'm not sure Roan realises I'm not talking about soccer, but her eyes light up all the same when I reminisce about what our Alpha was like when we were younger.

"What he's not telling you is that I only had two things on my mind, football and one geeky boy from my homeroom class who was obsessed with space movies."

"Obsessed?" I sputter. "I believe the word you're looking for is *connoisseur*."

"C'mere Roan." Our Omega happily sidles up to Clay. He wraps his arms possessively around her hips as he whispers in her ear.

"I'm sorry, what was that?" I know he's telling her something that is absolutely going to rile me up, and I can't wait for it. My tail's wagging about a mile a minute just wondering about what he's saying.

Roan's gaze flicks to mine over the table, a little sparkle behind them. Whatever Clay told her, it was juicy.

"I've been told that there is a costume."

My face heats as she looks at me. Clay really cut me deep with that one. I love a good cosplay or a reason to dress up. I know the guys down at the game shop play tabletop games, but I'm a space cowboy sort of nerd. I don't want to slay dragons when I could be saving alien babes. My Commander Arlak costume is peak alien babe, but what if Roan thinks I'm too weird?

"But more importantly, can we please talk about how ridiculous it was that they cut the romance from *Planet Pteranodon: Invasion of Tentacles*?"

My mouth drops open. She knows about the Ptera-verse. Holy shit!

"I know!" I gasp. "Tentacle erasure. Those aliens felt love."

Clay's gaze is smug as he watches Roan gush about her favourite space movies like he's heard me do a thousand times. Hell, I'm struggling to keep my boner concealed while she explains how she painted a whole series at school dedicated to the films. It's easy getting lost in the lore of my favourite series with Roan. Every odd little fact I've memorised gets her all the more excited.

"What's your favourite faction, Clay?" she asks him at one point, when things are getting a bit wound up between us.

"As the guy who attached ten billion rhinestones to that costume, if I'm not in Arlak's cyborg platoon, I will quit being his assistant."

Roan's eyes go all big and soft when he says it, and I've never felt luckier in my whole life.

Clay is everything I could have ever wanted in an Alpha and life partner.

My finger curls into his belt loop, and I pull him in for a soft kiss. Roan leans on her fist with this adorable, lusty, awestruck look on her face, and it's on the tip of my tongue to ask her what that look is for. But I don't need to.

The moment she gets the chance, she pulls Clay down and kisses him on the cheek. His jaw goes slack, and his grip on her hip loosens enough that she slips free of his hold. I've only got a second before she buries her small hands in my furry neck to kiss me too. Her breath tickles my whiskers right before the press of her lips meets my cheek.

"Let's keep dancing. I feel like I'm finally getting the steps." She bounces a little when a new song starts up, taking both of us by the hand to drag us out onto the floor.

Clay takes the lead now, twirling us around the scuffed floor and keeping us in line for the two-step. When the night blurs between laughter and gentle caresses, the band starts playing something with less boogie and more hip swing. Roan's body presses between ours, my hands resting on her soft hips while her arms are slung over Clay's shoulders. The heat of her body teases mine, making my cock dream of being buried somewhere hotter and wetter.

It's not often I feel an urge to be a top, but with our Omega I want it, need it. As she presses her ass into me, I look at Clay. His eyes are hungry, staring down at our mate. They flick to me, and I feel his stare like a brand on my heart. Our Omega, our mate, our pack.

"You keep working your little body like that, darlin', and we're gonna have to take you home now," I groan in her ear, fingers flexing into her plush, giving hips. It's not polite or discreet, but I grind a little into her too, so she knows what she's doing to me.

Her head falls back onto my shoulder, and she inhales the base of my neck. Just like it did a few days ago, the act of her scenting me goes right to my fucking dick.

"Then let's go home."

Chapter Thirteen

Clay

I TURN THE TRUCK down the side road behind the café and pull into our usual spot. Roan and Mitch have been talking almost nonstop about movies. Their voices are soft and easy while the cab soaks in the combined smell of all of us. It's like one big blueberry cake, layered with tangy sweet jam and thick vanilla buttercream. Waves of pride and desire rumble through me with every excited whisper they share. Our pack all squished together like this is how it's supposed to be.

Mitch helps Roan out of the truck, giving her a twirl around the gravel. Roan giggles, but then it's cut short. I turn and see my mates kissing. Without me.

Her fingers twist into his shirt to pull him down harder while he presses her into the side of the truck. He moans into her, winding his finger through her hair, and her clip falls off onto the hood.

Fuck me if that ain't the hottest thing I've ever seen. I adjust my dick, my knot swelling as I watch them. Their need for each other is taking over all our common sense.

"Clay," Roan whimpers into the night sky when Mitch kisses down her neck. "Please."

I move to their sides, pressing into my Beta to make sure he is surrounded on all sides by his pack. My chin hooks over Mitch's shoulder and I stare into our Omega's heavy eyes. She licks her lips, staring at me while Mitch is surely leaving the hickey of all hickeys. He's tried giving them to me in the past, the possessive side of him determined to make sure everyone knows his mate is taken and well cared for. All our fur hides claim marks, but nothing makes me nut harder than when he bites down hard.

"How can I help you, sugar?" I smirk, grinding into Mitch's ass, pressing his dick harder into her soft stomach.

"Want you," she whimpers with that same little pout.

Her bottom lip pushes out enough to make me fall a little bit faster and harder for her. My heart stutters as I lean around Mitch, who's more than eager to have our Omega overwhelmed by us. My snout catches on her nose with her haste and I love it. I do. I can't believe someone as gorgeous as our mate is rushing to get to me.

Roan huffs and grabs a hold of my shirt collar.

"Kiss me now," she demands.

"Omega, you've got a lot to learn about our Alpha," Mitch huffs, pushing back against me until he's leaning against the side of the truck and able to see us both.

I brace my arm on her other side, nodding in agreement. Nobody is bossing me around, in the bedroom or otherwise. I am happy to let people do as they please, but when it comes to my pack, having that extra bit of control centres something in my soul that I can't give up.

"Alpha?" She wrinkles her nose up, a sourness coming off her scent. "Is that one of those bro things?"

"No," I assure her. "It's a relationship dynamic thing. Do you like roleplay, Roan?"

We both look at her now, trying to guess what's running through her mind while she holds us in suspense. I know she's not had the exposure that we've had, and there will be a learning curve—if she's interested at all.

"Um, a little," she admits. Her gaze is laser focused on the button of my shirt that's undone. "Could we talk about this later and go back to having a threesome?"

I look at Mitch and sigh. "No, sugar. I know we're all hot and heavy, but it's good for us to know where you're at."

"And what we can do to make you comfortable and horny," Mitch adds, grabbing one of her hands to hold.

"I've never had *sex*-sex," she mumbles. "Not like, with other people."

"What do you mean?" I ask, trying to sound calm.

Holy fucking shit. We need to take this ten fucking steps back. Our Omega is a virgin and all we've done is treat her like a cheap date. I know Roan's an adult, but Mitch and I have years on her, over a decade.

"Do you still want to come upstairs?" Mitch must see my internal panic. "No pressure. We can drive you back to Connie's if you'd rather."

Roan rolls her eyes at him. "I'm not some eighteen-year-old losing her virginity to her hot older neighbours. Don't belittle me."

"Hey, now." I take a step to the side so we've all got a bit more cool, fresh air between us. "We're not trying to belittle you. We want you in our pack, Roan, we want to show you a good time, but we want it on your terms."

"Clay and I have known each other since we were pups on the football field. He still courted me for months just to make sure we were happy with how it worked," Mitch says.

"And I'd do it again for him all over, if he felt like our dynamic wasn't working. Just 'cause fate matched us together, don't mean we're instantly perfect."

Roan's eyes are big with fear and wonder. She chews her bottom lip for a moment, looking between us. I know what I'd do in her boots, but I don't want to influence her. My tail knocks against Mitch when it looks like he might start talking again.

"What if I don't like what you like?" she whispers. "What if what works for me doesn't work for one of you?"

"That's what conversation is for, but I'd be lying if I said we won't like anything you put on the table. As you so kindly pointed, darlin', we're old." Mitch cracks a smile. "There ain't much we haven't tried."

"A threesome?" She looks at us seriously.

"Nope, it's only ever been the two of us," I admit, gaze unwavering.

"Can we go inside now?" she asks.

Mitch leads the way, and I follow behind Roan as we head up the back stairs and into our tiny studio. I flick on a lamp and illuminate the space with a warm glow. It's not much, but looks like even less with Roan in here. Maybe it's because I've got that Alpha itch to let my Omega take over our space, smothering her scent all over everything and telling us which walls need to be repainted to make her happy.

Or maybe it's because she's probably never had to stay in a room so small in her life. I bet her bedroom back in London was bigger than our whole apartment.

"Oh, this is nice," she murmurs, heading over to the singular chair by our window. Mitch's sticky notes are still there in a heart shape. Her fingers brush over one of them as she looks at the full extent of our apartment. "It smells good."

"Were you expecting a wet bachelor smell?" Mitch teases.

He flops onto the bed while I sit on the edge, the mattress dipping under my weight. One of his hands sneaks around my back and strokes the base of my tail to relax me.

"No, but there's something more about how your house smells. It's more you." She inhales deeply and breathes out a heavy sigh.

That loosens a knot in my chest I didn't even realise formed there. She likes how our home smells. Even if it doesn't make much sense to her, that means the world to me. Our scents have saturated into every inch. It's our safest place.

"Explain the difference between sex and sex-sex," I say. "Is this like a young people difference between talking and dating?"

Both Roan and Mitch snort at my question.

"I mean, I've had a dildo for a long time, but another person hasn't like, fucked me." She tries to say it without showing off how embarrassed she clearly is to admit that. "I'm very goal-oriented and didn't have much time or interest in exploring."

"This ain't an interview, Roan." Mitch sits up, which really only makes it look more like an interview.

"Do you still want to have sex with us?" I ask.

"Yes," she answers without hesitation, leaning forward to be nearer us.

"Then let's make it fun and educational. We'll ask questions, and with every answer you get right, I'll take something off you or Mitch."

"Oh, I can be hot for teacher," my Beta laughs.

"Let's start easy then, do you know what a knot is, sugar?"

"Yes. It's a biological function designed to lock a penis-having being to another during intercourse to ensure reproduction."

"She paid more attention in biology than you did," I snort at Mitch.

"Look, my mama didn't say I'd have one. I wasn't expecting it," he laughs.

When a Wolven has sex after our second puberty, when we've presented as our designation of Alpha, Beta, or Omega, our knots pop for the first time. They're supposed to be a sign of sexual maturity and shit, but when you're an idiot in love, it's a bit of a surprise when it looks like two ping-pong balls appear on either side of your dick while your ass is spread wide open on your mate's much larger knot.

"Gimme your foot," I grunt, pulling off Mitch's boots and setting them over by the closet.

"Oh, I've got a question," he says with a wiggle of his toes. "What's your dildo like?"

"Does that really matter?" I ask, taking off my own boots in the shadow of our wardrobe so neither of them see me bend over.

"It's a Demon cock replica," she answers, a little flustered. "The knot vibrates."

"Fancy, fancy," Mitch hums, a little sparkle in his eye when he looks over at me.

Yeah, yeah, I get it. The question did matter. So she's not just fucking some pencil-thin G-spot stimulator. Roan has worked herself up to heavier equipment, which means my size won't be such a shock.

I move to kneel in front of her and begin unlacing her boots. She holds her breath while I do the first one, her shaky exhale worrying me. This is definitely not how Mitch and I started out, but I don't want to misstep with her. She's our Omega, someone we've been waiting for and dreaming about for a very long time.

Once her boots are tucked out of the way, I look up at her. The light reflects off the glitter on her skin, and I'm struggling to control my instincts. The ones that are hollering and carrying on that it's time to fuck our Omega into submission and keep her tied to our bed.

"Can I kiss you?" she whispers.

"What's the magic word, sugar?" I tease, even if her question makes my heart flutter with anticipation.

"Please, Clay." She's already leaning forward, and the material holding her neckline tight stretches dangerously right in front of my eyes. Her heavy cleavage threatens to spill right out, but my eyes are glued to her lips, and we kiss at last.

They're buttery soft and smooth against mine. My hands slide up her knees, spreading them a little wider as I push closer to her. She licks into my mouth first, little human tongue delving right in without fear of my sharper teeth. Fuck, she tastes good, and as she wraps her arms around my neck, I almost forget what we're doing here. I wrap my paw around the back of her neck and slowly ease her back. My thumb massages tight tendons, and Mitch's little marks that are starting to blossom.

"Do you like being taken care of?" I ask, voice a little huskier.

"Y-yeah." She hesitates, breaking eye contact with me.

I direct her back to my gaze, moving my other hand up her thigh. "Ain't nothing to be ashamed of, Roan. You work hard, you deserve to be spoiled a little."

"All that effort to show up those busybodies deserves to be rewarded," Mitch says, crowding around us. He's not one to be left out of a conversation, but I notice he's taken off his shirt and his jeans now. The tent in his boxers is right at our eye level. Now is not the time to be crotch-first.

"Sit down, Beta," I growl softly.

He groans a little, and only once I hear him flop back on to the bed do I continue.

"I like taking care of my people. Being a bit bossy is a part of my biology and my personality. As an Alpha, I'm most content when I know what I'm saying is being heard and my instructions followed."

Roan nods in understanding, leaning into my touch more, even as her eyes flick back behind me to Mitch.

"Do you think you can follow my lead, Omega?"

Chapter Fourteen

Roan

THIS ISN'T LIKE ANYTHING I've seen or heard about. I'm aware of the basics of BDSM in an ephemeral sense. I shared my studio space with a photographer who was really into Shibari and body contortion for a while. She gave the same talk to every model before a session. I had it practically memorised at one point.

Consent is everything, and one word can end the scene.

On a fundamental level, I get what Clay is telling me. He's a Dom, or Alpha, I guess, but it doesn't sound like he and Mitch ever stop having a scene. Their nature has led to them having a certain dynamic and expectation around their whole life. What if I can't live up to that?

"Do I get a safeword?"

"'Course." He nods. "You can also just say no at any point. We don't usually play that rough."

"Mine's *jelly*," Mitch offers. "Short and easy."

"Then can I say *toast*?" I ask. "I want to have sex, and I want to try this, but all the time sounds like a lot."

"We don't use our titles or designations outside of the pack," Mitch explains. "Clay only refers to me as Beta when we're alone. It's meant to be something special, just for us. We're not trying to make you act any different than you already do, Roan. It's more like we want you to turn it up a notch, when it's just us."

How do I already act?

In my head, there are two sides of me. The one that sounds more like my mother telling me I'm nothing more than a spoiled little girl. And the one where I know I've worked fucking hard to get where I am. The one that is confident in my choices and hopeful for the long, successful future ahead of me. All the time I spent practising, all the time I spent making mistakes, have led to my greatest adventure here in Hallow's Cove.

I want to be the version of me that's fearless. Clay and Mitch have been amazingly honest with me tonight, let me geek out and dance badly without any worry I'd be judged for it. If I'm honest with myself, I want nothing more than everything they are offering me right now. My body and soul are hungry for them.

"Roan, sugar." Clay's voice is thick, washing over me like a hot shower after a long day. "You still in there?"

"Sorry, sorry," I apologise quickly. "Did you ask a question?"

"Do you still want to do this, with us?" he asks.

"Yes, please." I grin.

Clay stands up first and offers me his hand. His rounded claws tickle my skin as he steps behind me. He slides the straps of my dress down, inch by inch, making all my hairs stand on end as his mate watches. Mitch cups his cock over his pants.

"You're so fucking beautiful, Omega," he whispers.

I look at all of him, thick fur wrapped around his muscular frame. Mitch looks like someone I want to sink my teeth into. "You're easy on the eyes yourself."

"Isn't he?" Clay whispers, unclasping my bra. "That pretty body is begging for attention."

I can't stop my sigh when my bra comes off. That thing is fucking irritating, but if I'm gonna dress nice, I've got to wear it. Mitch lets out a little whimper as Clay touches me. His fingers smooth down my arms, gently tracing my tattoos.

He glides his fingers over my apron belly without any hesitation, squeezing it as he pulls me a little tighter into him.

"Here's what I want to happen tonight," he says, kissing my neck. "I want you to tease our Beta while I get a taste of your perfect pussy."

My breath hitches. Are my nipples hard? Am I that hot already? Yes. Yes, I am. Mitch is practically panting on the bed, his tail thumping against the duvet as he takes his boxers off.

"When you're nice and wet for us, Omega, then we're going to see just how Mitch compares to your fake knot."

"What about you?" I ask, turning my head to look back at Clay.

He's still dressed. He hasn't even taken his shirt off. I know his body's excited, I can feel how hard he is against my low back. But his plans don't seem to include his pleasure. Does he not want us to touch him?

"I want to see you too," I push a little when he doesn't answer me.

"Alpha?" Mitch joins in, a little worry in his voice now too. "What can we do for you?"

"You think you can handle my knot while you fuck our girl?" he asks.

"Oh, the hardship." Mitch throws an arm over his face dramatically, and I giggle. "However shall we manage, darlin'? To have our Alpha on top of us, pushing us closer together, ruining our holes."

"I like the idea of a chain," I say, more to Clay than Mitch. "I want you both."

"Then get to work."

Clay taps my ass lightly as I crawl into their big bed. I've got half a mind to make a face at him, but once I'm in arm's reach, Mitch takes full control.

He kisses me with the same passion as he did outside, all tongue and teeth and eagerness that has me moaning into his mouth. His cock presses into my tummy, hotter and wetter than I imagined it would be.

Will it taste different than I imagined?

It's a struggle to pull myself back from our kiss, to let go of his fur enough that I can kiss down the rest of him. I've given one sort of blowjob in my life, to a Cecaelia I went on a date with. But that was more sucking her tentacle while she used one of her suction cups on my clit.

This is different. One, Mitch doesn't have any suckers to get caught on my teeth. Two, this experience hopefully won't end with only one of us finishing. I've learned I want my partners to take pleasure with me, from me, and not just me from them.

And the bit of fluid dribbling down Mitch's dick tells me he wants pleasure too. He's a decent size, a little less girthy than my dildo, which is probably good. His shaft is red and slick all the way down to where his knot swells just above his sheath.

"Ass up for me." Clay's husky voice reminds me I'm not just here to stare at some beautiful anatomy, but to enjoy.

I arrange myself on my hands and knees, letting Clay take my knickers off. I glance at Mitch as I kiss the very tip of his shaft.

"Keep going, darlin'. I'm all yours right now," he encourages.

I lick up the pre-cum from his dick, tasting the salty, savory flavor of him. He jerks when my tongue swirls around his knot, hips stuttering for place to slam into.

The ghost of Clay's breath across my thighs makes me tense. He spreads my ass cheeks and both of them groan in unison.

"You smell so fucking good, Omega," Clay murmurs. "So wet and pretty."

"I want it all over our bed, Alpha. Make a mess," Mitch says.

His fingers move to my hair, a suggestive tug at first, until he's gathered it in his fist to guide me down onto his cock. I swallow his tip just as Clay spreads my pussy lips farther apart with his fingers. Hot breath fans across my wet skin, and then his tongue flicks against my clit.

Oh, fuck.

My arms shake with how good it feels. It's almost easy. I know what I'm supposed to do, I know what they want me to do, and I'm getting what I want. Mitch moans as I swallow his dick, the gentle hand in my hair helping me find the tempo he likes. Clay licks and teases me, fucking his tongue little by little into my dripping pussy.

It's so easy to turn my brain off. I close my eyes, letting my other senses take the lead. My heart pounds so hard, I feel my pulse in my clit. The heady weight of my Beta's cock on my tongue grounds me while my Alpha's mouth shoots electricity right through my veins.

Is sex always like this? Can it always be like this?

"Fuck," Mitch shouts, pulling my mouth off him.

Drool and pre-cum dribble down my lips as I moan. My brain is on cloud nine right now, swimming in desire.

"Damn, lookachta, so gorgeous, Omega," Mitch pants. His dick is still hard, but he won't let me suck it again. "Focus on Alpha, he wants you to come for him."

As if to emphasise that, Clay moans against my pussy. My arms give out and I fall against Mitch's pelvis. Every breath I suck in now is mixed with the smell of his arousal. It's intoxicating.

The closer I get to orgasm, the higher I am from the warm scent of him.

"That's it, darlin', so good for us. Relax, let yourself finish. You can do that for us."

"Yes," I whimper, voice strained with need. "Please, Clay."

At my words, he grips my ass harder. A thrill cuts through my hazy desire, and I realise just how close I am. My body shakes with need and my lower stomach tightens.

"Don't stop, don't stop," I chant as he sucks on my clit.

I shout when I come. My hips jerk hard and my legs shake as my pussy convulses against Clay's face. He keeps suckling until I'm pulling away, completely overwhelmed.

"Oh, I think you're in trouble, sugar," he groans. "Going to have to keep you pinned right here, feasting on your pussy every day."

"If it always feels this amazing, I won't complain," I groan, not ready to move just yet. Mitch pets my hair as I level out, trying to catch my breath. His hard cock bobs right next to my face.

"You want more?" he finally asks.

"I'm all yours."

Chapter Fifteen

Mitch

It takes every ounce of my concentration to not come, to not let the short, panting breaths of my sated Omega throw me over the edge of orgasmic oblivion. Next time, maybe I will. Next time, when Clay fucks her good and hard, I'll let her moans and their wet bodies slapping together be the only thing that brings me over the edge.

But right now, I need to focus. I'm about to feel what a pussy feels like for the first time. I've fucked Clay before, so I'm not completely in the dark about what this is going to feel like, but I'm suddenly nervous.

What if Roan thinks I'm bad at this?

Clay puts us how he wants us, arranging us sideways across the bed so it doesn't squeak like I hate. We should really just buy a new bed, but our mattress is massive and it was a fucking pain to get all this up here. He places two of our pillows below our Omega's hips so any of her arousal has a chance to mark her scent for each of us.

Her body relaxes, her skin stretches and gives in all her soft places as she lies before me like a feast. The deep valley and soft rolling hills that make up the planes of her form call to me on a primal level. I want to explore every inch of her. My dick pulses when I look at her naked and spread out for us. She looks right like this in our bed. Like she's supposed to be here.

"Oh, I've got condoms in my bag," she says, pushing herself up on an elbow.

I'm glad one of us is thinking.

"Thank you, sugar." Clay smiles as he goes searching for that tiny clutch.

We haven't used condoms in such a long time, any that we have still hanging around are surely dust by now. We've just opted to use those mail-order tests regularly and then get the big screening done when we have annual physicals. It's a bit expensive, but I get anxious, even if we are monogamous.

"We tested about a month ago," I assure her. "Nothing to report."

"I got my implant replaced over the summer, and they did a screening. It's all good, but I—"

"We want you to be comfortable, Omega. A little latex isn't going to hurt my feelings."

Roan places her hands over her face as her cheeks burst with a blush.

"What?" I lean over, my wet cock dragging across her tummy as I pull her hands free.

"It's just really hitting me," she murmurs. "This is real, and we're doing this."

"You're packed up, Omega," Clay says with a hint of humour in his voice as he comes up behind me with a fist full of supplies.

She doesn't say anything, focusing instead on all the goodies our Alpha brought to bed. Condoms, lube, dilator, wet wipes, snacks, and a fresh glass of water, all the essentials carefully set within arm's reach. He opens the condom, but rather than handing it over, he gets behind me.

A shiver runs down my spine as he cups my balls, and I can't decide if it's because I'm on fire or if it's our audience. Roan's eyes are glued to my dick. She watches as Clay tortures me, squeezing with a firmer hand and pulling my sheath a little further back than necessary. I moan, leaning into his grip and the pleasure that comes with it. He grips the base of my shaft hard as he rolls the bright yellow condom down and over my knot.

"Now be good to our girl," he instructs. "And I'll be good to you."

"Fuck," I mutter.

"What?" Roan asks, a hint of concern in her voice.

"I promise, darlin', I promise," I say, placing one of my hands by her head while I use my other to caress her side. "I will try not to come before you do."

Her eyes go big for a moment. "Okay..."

Clay lies over my back, his furry belly moulding the curve of my spine as I flick my tail to the side and feel his cock rub against my hole. He reaches around me, his hand taking hold of Roan's hip and better lining us up. My tip slides through her labia, nudging against her clit until she's gripping my shoulder and moving on her own. The smell of blueberries and pastries takes over me.

Gods, I'm so fucking hungry for them. Am I even going to survive this?

"What you've got to know about our Beta, sugar." Clays voice is thick with passion as he reveals what a fucking goner I am. "He can talk a big game all he wants, but he's an easy, needy boy who can't hold back when he's feeling good."

Roan's lips form a little O before she smiles like a million bright lights at me.

"It's okay," she says. "We can be easy together."

A hoarse laugh comes out of me. Shit, I might be in love all over again. Clay pulls back and I hear the lube cap pop. I focus on my Omega beneath me. The hands on my shoulders dig into my fur when I tease her nipple. I pluck at one softly, watching the soft bud harden in my touch. She arches her back and the tip of my cock slips into her warm, wet pussy.

"Yes, more," she whines.

Fuck, fuck, fuck. I need to breathe or I'm going to blow my load right now. Roan feels so good, even with just a small part of me inside her. I can feel her desire, her need, pulsing around the head of my dick. Clay grabs the base of my tail and I tense as pleasure shoots through me.

"You heard her, sunshine." He growls playfully, a nip at my ass cheek to get me to buck my hips.

My shaft buries right to my knot in one slick stroke. Roan shouts with pleasure, and I grit my teeth to keep from coming. I pause, breathing sharply through my nose just in case the noise was too much for Clay. He doesn't hesitate, slipping the narrow tip of the toy into my ass. We should have done more prep, but I'm not sure I would have been able to focus on anything else while we were out if I'd worn a plug.

Each of my breaths are laboured and harsh as my body shakes. As I pull out of Roan, I sink deeper onto the dilator for Clay.

"Fuck," I whimper, thrusting forward again and again in a punishing chase for release.

I want to be knot-deep in Roan's warm, wet pussy. I want to feel our Alpha's hips bounce off my ass. I need to feel her clench around me when I stroke just the right spot. I need his cock teasing my prostate every time he thrusts into me.

More than anything, I want to feel overwhelmed by them both, completely surrounded and drowning in the scents while we're locked together and sated. Clay pulls the toy out of me like he can read my thoughts, or maybe he's just as desperate to get to the next part of his master plan, but either way, I know I'm never going to forget this first.

Roan's eyes shine when she meets my gaze. Her cheeks are flushed a deep red all the way down to her tattoo-covered chest, the patchwork pieces of art jiggling every time I get a bit closer to fucking my knot into her. She tugs me down for another kiss, licking into my mouth in hungry need for more of me. How did I get so lucky?

"So perfect, Omega," I groan when I nearly slip my knot inside her. "What do you need? I want you to feel good."

"Want your knot, Beta," she says, words tinged with desperation.

"He'll give it to you, sugar," Clay rumbles behind me.

My brain is gone. Offline. Useless until further notice.

Roan called me Beta.

The tip of Clay's dick is solid and wet, easing into my asshole like it's my first time too. I whine, not because of the heavy stretch, but because I'm easy. I crave more from my Alpha and Omega. My singular focus is on them, on me.

"Alpha," I whimper, my claws digging into the bedding, into Roan's plush hips. I clench, letting all the buzzy, tingling feelings slip from my fingertips right into my balls and aching knot. "I'm close."

"Me too." Roan's fingers release my fur.

She squeezes her hand down between us. Her body is slick with sweat, her hair clinging to her forehead. Roan is the most beautiful Omega I have ever seen. Fitting into our dynamic without trying. In the back of my mind, I know tomorrow will bring more discussion and negotiation and all the other work that comes with pack.

But right now, it's all just feeling good.

Her pussy tightens around my shaft as she touches her clit. My arms shake with the effort to hold back, to not orgasm right then.

"Relax, Beta." Clay's words are soothing against my ear as he presses completely into me, pushing me deeper into Roan.

His hands wrap around mine. He tightens my grip on Roan, her lips parting at the sting of pain.

"Yes," she whimpers. "Fuck me."

Clay takes over. Our Alpha fucks us, thrusting hard enough the bed shakes. I don't care. If we break the bed with how feral we are our first time, I'll never be more proud. My hindbrain, drowning in the smell of my mates, is giddy at the chance to show our Omega what aggressive and dominant Wolven we are. How good we are together.

My lips part, but no words come out, not even babbling nonsense. I've never been speechless before.

"Look what your sweet pussy does to him, Omega," Clay grunts. His knot teases my hole, stretching and stretching with each hard thrust. "Fuck, look what it's doing to me."

There's a single beat before he fucks his knot into me, forcing my knot into Roan. Clay's knot presses hard against my prostate as he cums and my body seizes, balls drawing in close and my knot swelling more than it ever has. He grinds into me, pushing my knot deeper into our Omega until she comes. Her pussy pulses around my knot, and my world goes white.

"Beta!" she cries.

Faintly, under the rushing of blood through my ears, I hear her. But my elbow collapses where it's holding me up, and I lose myself.

Chapter Sixteen

Clay

I BLINK THROUGH THE stars behind my eyes, focusing on the limp body hanging off my knot and the panting, whimpering noises from underneath Mitch. His ass is cinched tight around my knot, swollen bigger than normal with the satisfied scent of our sated Omega drenching our bed. Mitch's face is pressed into her neck, where he's breathing heavily. He twitches, hips thrusting a fraction in an erratic pattern.

Roan's got tears in her eyes.

"Sugar, look at me," I rumble, drawing on sound deep in my chest. Her eyes meet mine, a little lost and unfocused. "Are you hurt?"

"No," she sniffles.

"Can I touch you?" I ask softly.

"Please," she whimpers again, eyes closing as tears slip free.

I slip my arm around all of us, my shoulder pulling hard at the stretch. I know in a few hours I'll be paying for it, but it doesn't matter. My Omega needs me. I roll us on our side. We're all still stuck together, and will be for a few more minutes, but this will help take the weight off her. The hand not trapped between her body and Mitch's reaches for me.

It's shaking as they grab hold of my fur, trying to pull me into her. I reach out to swipe away the tears, and she huffs.

"So unsexy."

"What is?"

"Crying," she says, sad humor in her voice. "Had the best time of my life and I—"

She chokes on a little sob, and Mitch wraps his arm tight around her waist. He is still too fucked out to wake up. I haven't taken him this deep in a long time, and I didn't think it would happen tonight, but the action does soothe Roan a touch more.

"Your brain is telling you to release all that euphoria," I try to explain. "It's kinda normal. We've both cried because the sex is that good."

She looks at me slowly drying eyes. "It was the best. You were amazing."

Her praise hits me in the chest, even if I feel it's slightly undeserved on my part. My knot twitches, shooting more cum into Mitch as my cheeks heat. Her tone is insistent though, like she won't hear anything else.

"You look so gorgeous, sugar," I say, turning the conversation back to her instead. "Perfect Omega."

"Yeah?"

I don't miss the way her voice dips, a slight uncertainty in her question. "Yeah, Roan. Words can't describe what you mean to us. Even if things don't go as planned, you'll still be perfect to us. Mitch and I are set on you, sugar. So long as you want us, you've got us."

There's a spike of sweet blueberries, and then the finger curls deeper into my arm. We lie in silence, but the more it stretches between us, the more something settles inside of me.

Maybe I didn't want to admit it before, but I'm scared. Now more than ever, I'm scared that I'm going to fuck this up and ruin two people's lives because I'm a horrible Alpha. When we'd tried dating, looking for an Omega who we could connect with, it hurt when it didn't work out. It was always mutual, always because our scents just didn't match.

But the three of us smell like we'd make the perfect bake.

I can't fuck this up.

"Alpha," Mitch grumbles, finally rousing enough from his fucked-out snooze. "You smell like burnt toast, stop it."

"Oh," Roan says. "I thought that was just in my head."

"Smells like that when he's being a dickhead," Mitch explains, nuzzling into Roan more while also shoving his ass back into me.

"I won't have none of that," she says.

"Such a good Omega," he praises her.

"It ain't gang up on your Alpha hour," I groan, my knot deflating quicker with my worry. It slips out of Mitch easily, cum leaking onto his furry cheeks. He and Roan both make a noise when his dick is released from her pussy, the condom hanging on for dear life now. I reach between them and gently peel it away to tie off. "Let's get cleaned up so we can cuddle."

"I call dibs on being in the middle," Roan says with a grin.

It's damn near impossible to drag myself out of bed a few hours later. Going forward, dates need to be in the afternoon. I require at least eight hours of sleep, so that when I wake up to my Omega's ass smooshed right against my hard dick when my alarm goes off, I get to savour it a bit rather than getting growled at by two grumpy mates. Both of them huff and snuggle into each other, not even waking up as I roll out.

As I throw on clothes, my heart screams at me to get back in bed. My fucking eyeballs are begging me to be shut for just a little longer. I'm exhausted, a zombie of a Wolven trying to force their meat suit to leave what could very well be my new pack's nest. Watching the two of them snore and cuddle in their own weird way makes me want to wrap them up in my arms and never work again.

But that's not how the world is. It doesn't stop moving, bills aren't forgotten, and people are still depending on us, even if we are a simple café.

I kiss each of my mates on the forehead and lock the back door as I leave.

Hallow's Cove is an odd place. I imagine in most towns, this early in the morning, it's quiet and deserted. But in the wee hours of the morning here, night school is ending and nocturnal monsters are rushing off to get a bite to eat before sunrise. Some shops down Main Street are closed, while others are still open. Ted's is perpetually open. I can't remember the last time they were closed completely.

The bright lights of the bakery's kitchen are especially blinding today when I start prepping. I set up my doughs that need to rest first, then move on to bakes that will need time to cool before I can place them on platters. Usually I try to make one new thing every day, something that will keep customers coming back other than my perfect pastries. As much as I like a schedule, a routine, I do have this one small creative bone in my body that likes to try new recipes. The troll I apprenticed with and eventually bought the café from left me an ancient book of recipes. Their handwriting is atrocious. Some of the recipes have faded with age or are covered in stains, and others are downright awful.

But for whatever reason, my tired brain decides today is the perfect day to break out one of these old recipes. I pull down the fireproof box I keep them in and start gingerly flipping through the pages. None of these scratch the itch I've got. Finally, I get so frustrated with that, I close the book and my eyes, and then open up to a random page.

"Siren's Lucky Nipple."

I can't be reading that right. It makes no sense, but there at the bottom of the page is a crude drawing of a boob shape with a berry pressed in the middle. Sometimes, I wonder if this thing is cursed. The recipe is clear enough though, so I pull out all the ingredients and to shape the boobs, I pull down my rarely used madeleine pan. That's almost what this recipe is, just with a more pervy name.

Following the recipe keeps me awake, though, vigilant to my timer and the need to open up the front door. Ted's face is pressed hard into the front glass as I step out of the kitchen. Eager bastard. I flick on half the lights and set up coffee to start dripping first, just to spite him. I'm going to have to wash that window now to make sure the imprint of his big face doesn't scare off customers.

"Wasn't sure you'd be open this morning." He winks at me as he comes in.

Jeremy follows closely behind, but goes to his regular table by the counter. He'll pay for his cup of coffee once Ted's secured his bread order for the day.

"Why wouldn't I do the same thing I've done for over a decade now?" I ask.

"You left your window open last night. Lerana overheard some...activities."

My ears flatten and my haunches rise.

What my pack does in our house is our fucking business. I don't want the whole damn town gossiping about my Omega or Beta having a nice time.

"Ted, watch yourself." It's all the words I can get out. I'm getting too emotional about this.

He raises his hands, pursing his lips like he's not going to tell the whole damn town about our date. We are a group of adults, all consenting. It's fine that people know we had a good time. But I saw Roan's reaction to the first bit of gossip Ted shared. She doesn't want people thinking ill of her.

"Just saying, might be good to keep it down."

As he says it, the faintest scent of blueberry pancakes walks through the front door. Roan's all wrapped up in my big flannel shirt from last night, her dress just peeking out from buttons she hasn't closed around her hips. She's not swimming in it, but the sleeves are so much longer than her short arms that it looks adorable and sexy all the same. Her unlaced boots clomp as she walks up to the counter, eyeing Ted.

"Morning," he says.

"You alright?" she asks.

"Yup, just reminding Clay about respecting his neighbour's peace and quiet." He doesn't wink at her the way he did me. It's not a playful insinuation. It's just fucking rude.

She doesn't flinch, doesn't look away from him when she makes a noise in the back of her throat. Thankfully, my timer goes off.

"That'll be your bread. Roan, can you help me for a second?" I ask because it's polite, but really I'm trying to tell her to come to the kitchen with me.

She smiles brightly when she looks at me, already heading behind the counter towards the door. I open the oven doors and pull out the tin loafs for Ted before I glance at my mate. She looks sleepy, but not exhausted. I wonder how long this jet lag stuff lasts if she still has hours like mine, but my question is forgotten when she wraps her arms around my waist.

"Morning," she whispers.

"You sleep okay?" I rub my hand up and down her back, inhaling our mixed scents.

"So okay." She smiles. "I feel like almost a whole person."

I cock my head to the side a little at that comment. What does that mean?

Maybe it would be worthwhile to wake Mitch up just so we can have our big pack meeting now rather than later. Clear all the air, make sure we are all happy, that we know what expectations we have for our relationship and that we all feel safe.

"Clay, you're either burning something, or you're thinking so hard your brains turned to toast again." She pokes my side, making me giggle of all fucking things until I release her.

Roan smiles at me, and the impending panic I feel fades away. She is right, though, something does smell too done. I pull open another oven door and yank the nipple cakes out of the oven.

Rather than being a soft light blue colour with one plump blueberry at the centre, the cakes are a little more purple with a black mark in the middle. Roan makes a noise of interest, gathering up her hair to lean over and smell them.

"These look incredible." She inhales again. "Are these for something special?"

"No, I just felt like making something a little different."

My Omega watches silently as I place a dozen loaves of bread into the paper flour sack I saved for Ted's order today. She seems content to simply sit and enjoy the view before her, which makes me more self-conscious than I thought it would. I take the bread out to Ted, pour Jeremy and myself a cup of coffee, then drop a tea bag into a mug of hot water for Roan. She perks up when I set the mug in front of her, her fingers tapping the hot ceramic as it brews. I pass her a milk carton, trying to gauge how big of a splash she likes before putting it away again. Hearing her sigh into that first sip is how I want to start every morning: my Omega content, smelling fresh and sweet while I work.

"Thank you for the tea," she murmurs after a little while. "I know it's a faff, but it means a lot."

"I don't know what that means, Omega. But I'll always do what I can to make you happy." I pull on a clean pair of gloves.

"What if I want one of your pirate cakes?" She looks from me to the cooling disasters and back again.

A smile creeps up my lips. I'm more than happy to oblige that request. I pull a small plate down and put two cakes on it for her. She makes a noise when I'm near her, turning her face up to mine. She's got that little sparkle in her eyes that's probably my imagination, but I love seeing it, seeing her all bright and happy.

"What can I do for you, sugar?"

"A kiss would be nice...please." She grins, tacking on that *please* almost sarcastically.

I smirk, unable to help myself either. I lean down until we're almost touching. Her hands flex around her mug, but I have to keep mine at my side. "What kinda kiss?"

Roans cheeks flush, but she doesn't miss a beat. "One that says *good morning, love, thank you for not glassing a customer this morning.*"

My shoulders shake with laughter, but I do as she requests. My lips meet her slowly, lazily, lingering and teasing all at once, until I hear the back door open.

"My kissing senses are right," Mitch huffs like a child who still wishes he was in bed. He's half-dressed, slippers on. I might make an earlier riser out of him yet, if it means he has no one to cuddle in the morning.

He shuffles over to Roan and kisses her. His hands wrap around the nape of her neck and she goes practically limp in his quick embrace. When Mitch is satisfied our girl is ravished, he promptly looks at me like I've offended him.

"*That* is how we kiss our Omega," he says.

I look down at the batch of pain au raisins I need to finish and strip my gloves off. Like hell will I be shown up. Roan's rosy cheeks look like fresh apples as she turns her gaze back to me, ready and waiting.

I slip one hand into her hair at the base of her neck and use the other to grip her chin. "Is that how you wanna be kissed, sugar? You want your Alpha to take your breath away before you've even had breakfast?"

"He should certainly try," she taunts, putting out that bottom lip.

Like the first kiss of the morning, I start off slow. I'm not going to rush our passion and hunger for each other when I know we can rut into oblivion. This is just stoking the coals for later, keeping everyone's blood a little hot for the work day. My tongue slips between her lips, and she whimpers. The press of her body into mine is so perfect, so soft and generous.

She blinks when I pull back, that dazed little look doing wonders for my confidence.

"Beta," I grunt.

I'm not faster with Mitch, not harder. My fingers grip his fur when I kiss him slow and deep. His tail thumps hard when I lick his mouth. Gods damn it. I'm teasing myself just as much as I am them.

He chases after me when I break our kiss.

"Don't tempt me, you two," I grumble. "No more threesomes until we have a thorough discussion."

Both of them groan, but I imagine it's for different reasons. Roan still seems anxious talking about her desires, and Mitch is always happier following gut instinct in personal matters, which has previously got us banned from the movie theatre two towns over.

His idea of making everyone comfortable is simply going with the flow, addressing an issue as it appears. I can't operate that way. We can't fuck around and find out how we all work best, especially not when our Omega's new to this.

I pull up a stool for Roan and Mitch gets his from behind the counter.

"Now," I say, pulling on another pair of gloves. "Let's talk wins and fumbles from last night."

Chapter Seventeen

Roan

You go on one amazing, fun, and hot as hell date and you get sent home with homework.

Homework!

I didn't even do this stuff when I was at school. Why does Clay have to be so mean? I'm completely fine with talking about how fucking hot and overwhelming it was to have my first time having real sex be a threesome. I can chat for days about how incredibly sexy it was watching Mitch lose his mind between me and Clay. I could spend all day on the pleasure I received from Clay's mouth. Hell, even when we had to talk about things we didn't think went well or things we want to change for next time, I was still on cloud freaking nine because, fuck me, I've got mates.

Not one, but two hot, older monster men who are secure in their relationship and eager to have me in it with them.

But being handed an extra paper cup that had a kink website and scribbled directions on it? Yeah. Not cool. Mitch promised me he'd give me a special treat if I filled out all the stuff that Clay asked. He also said they'd both done it as well once they got more into the BDSM side of their relationship, and did more internal work on how their Wolven instincts affected their bond.

They didn't give me a timeline for this homework, and I'm not exactly jumping for the chance to use the decrepit "business centre" at the motel. Connie said the original setup was state of the art, but I think they still have a fax machine next to the giant box they call a computer. That's going to have to be a midnight rendezvous when I know there are no eyes open to peek over my shoulder.

I need to focus on the Cove Arts Centre. That's my purpose for being here. Rick came around two days ago with all the supplies I ordered, so I've got plenty to keep me busy. Just like with the clear-out, I start on the ground floor. I'm potentially in over my head, clambering up and down the ladder scrubbing the walls and ceiling clean so I can paint them once they're dry.

The floors are a different subject. I need a builder to manage that, but for getting this place up and operational, a lick of paint will do. My arms ache by the early afternoon. The cleaning jumpsuit I changed into after Mitch dropped me off at the motel is soaked.

The ground floor is clear, though, and I had hoped I'd be able to do the first floor today as well, but I don't think that's going to happen. I run up to the loft, panting by the time I'm there, and I strip completely out of this suit.

I throw it over the railing outside to dry in the waning sunshine.

An afternoon of sketching will be good for my soul. There are a few things I want to add to my goals list as well. I want to have monthly art nights here at the centre, something to get tourists and townspeople excited to come here. There is nothing more oppressive and ostentatious than an empty gallery.

My phone lights up with a call from my agent.

We didn't part on the best terms after my last show. I'd had only one request for opening night, and my mother showing up unannounced meant they weren't really the sort of business partner I was looking for.

"Hey, Zee, you alright?" I answer after too many rings.

"So you are alive, Rowena." My mother's clipped tone in the receiver takes my brain offline. "You have one poor showing, and you spiral into this nonsense. I had to force this tiny Fae to hand over their even tinier mobile just to get in contact with you. They said you've gone off the rails, taken some 'boggin' backwater residency in a dump."

Okay, maybe I was mean enough. Hallow's Cove is a diamond in the rough, rich with a community that can't be replicated anywhere else.

"What do you want, Mum?" I ask instead.

"Your brother has...stepped out of line, and we need you to come home."

"What?" I stutter.

My brother is a cherubic shining light to our household. Camberford educated and the future Marquis of Farrador, Donovan has always been the child my parents praise the most, love the most. He's never done a single thing wrong in his life. How the fuck could he have fallen so far that they want me back?

"You know how it is," Angelica insists. "Some spineless paparazzo takes a photo they shouldn't have and now the rags are trying to bleed us for pence. It's really all very ridiculous."

"Excuse me?" My voice rises. Every hair on my body stands on end at her implication.

"Oh, it's just some media spin. We just need to turn it back in our favour. Your flight's already booked, bobble, just head to the airport in the morning." She continues on like she isn't asking me to just abandon everything here.

I'm going to be sick. She can't be serious. Donovan is entitled. He thinks he can do whatever he likes, but he's not stupid enough to do something illegal in front of those cretins. What on earth could have gotten Lady Angelica so riled about this?

It doesn't matter. They won't use me to cover up his slip, whatever it is. I've barely spoken to him since he went off to uni, too busy networking to pay attention to his younger sister. Donovan is a grown man. His mistakes or public slips are his own to deal with, not mine.

"No." I scowl at my trembling hand, still gripping my pencil.

"No? Rowena, I refuse to fight two scandals on different continents. You will come home tomorrow and you will play the part you were born to." Her voice rises to meet mine.

"Or what?" I say, calling her bluff. She can't possibly do anything else to hurt me more than that review.

There is a pause on the line, the only sound is the blood rushing through my ears. I can't even imagine what she's doing at this very moment. Her calm facade sounds shattered over the line. She doesn't expect me to refuse or fight when she gives me a command.

"We'll disown you," Mum finally says. "No more connections, no more allowance, you will be completely cut out of the family and everything we have given you."

My brow furrows at that. I don't use those now. I've done everything I can not to use my family's influence.

"What are you talking about?"

"Do you truly believe I haven't been paying for your lifestyle? Oh, bobble." She says that godsawful nickname like I'm some stupid idiot. "What artist do you know who gets monthly stipends? Who has patrons in this economy?"

No.

"Your father and I figured you would grow out of this once you'd found a husband we preferred. We didn't mind indulging you while you weren't causing a fuss, but now you are."

Tears fall down my cheeks before I can stop them.

"So you have a choice, come home tomorrow and be the sort of daughter we can be proud of, or don't bother speaking to us again."

The line cuts.

Has it all been a lie, then? My lungs pump like I'm gasping for air, but nothing is coming in. A sob, choked and weak, comes out of me. The thoughts in my head morph, taking on the voice of my mother. Every critique, every reprimand, every backhanded remark comes bubbling up to the surface, and I can't stop crying.

Zephyr had been happy when they negotiated that deal with the anonymous patron, some angel investor for the arts. I felt so lucky finding that East London studio for a bargain. It had felt like pieces falling into place, before my mother's terrible review of my first solo show.

Everyone in Hallow's Cove is right. I'm a fraud and a failure.

I really thought I was making myself into a better person, but it was just a lie.

Chapter Eighteen

Mitch

THE FIRST DAY WE don't see Roan, I chalk it up to her being busy. The Arts Centre is a big project. The second day, I can't stop staring out the window at that building, hoping I'll catch a glimpse of her so I can run over. Clay ruins a patch of blueberry muffins on the third day. I catch him crushing one of the burnt pastries in his hand as he throws them away, angry tears in his eyes. I drive the truck down to Connie's to see if she's around, but Roan isn't there.

As if this past week hasn't been stressful enough with Roan ghosting us, this month's town hall meeting is in absolute shambles over nothing. It smells like burnt toast, and I'm not sure if I'm having a stroke from how fucking stupid some of these people are or if Clay really, really is that close to burning the whole damn town hall to the ground.

And it's raining tonight, so everyone's dripping wet.

Mayor Louise sits at the front of the hall behind a rickety old folding table. On either side of her are Lerena, who's taking furious notes, and Barnaby, who looks ready to die from boredom. We have these same conversations every month. It's always the same. Here's what tourist-driving festival we're having this month, there's what programs the schools are putting on, here's another load of crap for us all to throw our time and money behind while we try to get the state tourism board to notice us.

Oh, and it smells like shit coffee in here.

This is truly the worst of all town hall meetings in history. I huff, tired and annoyed and just damn pouty, when Louise mentions wanting to do something classier this winter to appeal to the ski bunnies. Apparently Andri's annual kegger does not count as classy in the eyes of the general population, but I always have a great time there.

"Oh, why don't we schedule something with the Arts Centre?" Lerena smiles jovially, like a lightbulb truly has just popped up between her small Faun antlers. "Is Roan here?"

There's a rumbling through the crowd as people turn in their seats to look for her. There are a few pointed stares directly at us, but Clay and I are looking around just as much as them. She's not in the crowd that I can see or smell.

"She's not here," Clay states clearly.

Barnaby's brow furrows in confusion, and his eyes flick to someone in the front row. Maisie will absolutely be hunting us down after this meeting if she doesn't already know what's going on.

"Are we surprised?" Ted asks. "Her ladyship couldn't lower herself to see us."

"Excuse you?" I shout, half out of my seat before Clay is pulling me down. "Don't talk about her like that."

He gives me a look that says we don't need to raise our voices. Shit. Fucking damnit. I squeeze his hand in apology, even if I want to get in a fucking shouting match with Ted.

We can defend our Omega without losing our cool.

"Well, shouldn't she be here? Aren't we paying her?" he demands, continuing on this interjection.

"She's probably at the Centre," Gnurl Lumzag points out. "She hasn't been at the motel much, too determined to get that place cleared out."

"Yeah, I dropped off a load of stuff for her last week," Rick confirms. "It's really coming together."

"Ted, to answer your question, she is receiving a small stipend through the city's budget," Louise confirms. "But it's nothing serious, barely above minimum wage."

"Hold the fucking phone." Clay stands up, suddenly baring his teeth. "You can't expect her to live off that. None of us can!"

There is a short round of applause for that comment, and it brings a bit of warmth to my heart knowing what kind of community we want here.

"Clay, I understand your concern, and she was fully aware of our budget constraints, even offering to take the role as a volunteer." Louise folds her hands over her notebook. "She truly just wanted to be a part of bringing back the arts here."

"Then where the hell is she?" Ted stands up, towering over a good portion of the crowd.

I don't know.

That's all I can think about. I don't know where our mate is, because every attempt we've made to contact her this week has failed. The lights have been on at the Arts Centre, but Connie says she hasn't been around the motel. My fingers slip into my hoodie pockets, feeling her handkerchief I've taken to carrying around, as worry gnaws at my gut.

Why isn't she speaking to us?

Everything seemed fine when we parted ways, when I drove her back to Connie's, when I reminded her to drink more than just tea all day. Was it me? Did I come on too strong?

"Attendance at these meetings isn't required," Louise reminds the crowd. "Now, we've got a lot of other business to handle tonight, so let's get to it."

And the meeting goes on. Clay sits back down, an unnatural scowl marring his face. He's been carrying so much weight this week. If it weren't for his firm grip on my hand, I'm not sure I'd be coping at all. We've weathered dark times before, but I don't know how much more we can be battered.

"Before we close out tonight's meeting, is there any final new business we'd like to bring up?"

There's a beat of silence, the rustling of people gathering their coats and umbrellas together, when there's a crash in the hall outside. Clay immediately scoots his chair in the way of mine. It's adorably protective, but I'm nosey. I want to see what's going on.

Roan bursts through the door, covered in white paint and looking like a drowned rat in a bicycle helmet.

"Is the meeting over?" she gasps, trembling fingers reaching around for her backpack.

"Not officially, Lady—I mean, Roan." Louise sits up a bit straighter when she sees my mate.

"I—" She clears her throat, trying to catch her breath while maintaining eye contact with no one as she steps forward towards the table. "I would like to propose a-a monthly class to begin at the Cove Arts Centre in two weeks' time."

No one speaks. We all just stare at her. I want to go to her, talk to her so we can understand. Clay holds a firm hand on my neck to keep me seated.

"The first floor of the gallery has been completely refurbished. While the ground and second floors are still in progress, I understand people are eager to see the work I've been doing," she explains.

"What sort of class?" Barnaby asks.

My jaw literally drops. This man hasn't spoken a word in these meetings in over a decade. Last time I can recall was in regards to bird migration and some sort of boob.

"I—I've got a list of potential options. Some are more ambitious than others, and I can happily email the full list to any committee member that needs to review it, um, but I believe starting with a simple charcoal life drawing class would have the most appeal."

"Oh, sounds fun," I hear Gwen from the game shop murmur.

"Girls' night," a purple-haired human whispers between her and the other human sitting next to her.

"This all sounds fine," Louise says. "But not like something we need to discuss here."

"I need to request a small budget for supplies," Roan insists, before the mayor can close the meeting. "And enough to pay the model fairly. I've got a proposal."

Roan shuffles forward and hands over a few soggy sheets of paper. Louise takes them, looks at them for two seconds, and shoves them back at Roan. They whisper something to each other, and damn, do I wish I had better hearing.

Our Omega sheepishly takes the papers back and hands the mayor a different set.

"200 for the model for three hours, 100 for paper, charcoal, and clipboards, and then a final fifty dollars for refreshments," Louise lists out.

"Yes, ma'am," Roan says, her voice trembling slightly.

"That's a total of $350." Lerena calculates the basic math.

The mayor looks out over the crowd like she's waiting for someone to speak. I'm waiting for Ted to be an ass, but he isn't. We all just sit in our seats like bumps on a log.

"I move to approve a budget of $350 to fund a monthly life drawing class at the art centre," Clay states firmly, like he's daring someone to disagree with him.

"I second it," Gwen says, raising her hand.

"Unless there are any arguments, I see no reason to hold off on voting on this motion." Louise pauses, but nowhere nearly long enough for Ted to speak. "All those in favour, say aye."

I would guess about eighty five percent of the room responds.

"Nay?"

There are three or four people who vote against it, but definitely not all the fifteen percent that didn't say *aye*.

"Great, motion passes. Roan, come by my office in a couple of days, and Lerena will get your expenses sorted."

"Meeting adjourned," Barnaby says quickly after that.

Before we can even stand up, he and his mate have surrounded Roan. Maisie grabs her by the shoulders while they exchange a quiet word. I wish I knew what it was about. I wish Clay wasn't anchoring me by the hall's gross coffee station so I could smell blueberries again.

No amount of baking could replace that scent for us. All week, Clay tried different blueberry recipes. Cakes, scones, crumble—none of it was right when the real thing was just out of reach.

Roan and Maisie hug a final time, and then she turns in our direction. Out of the corner of my eye, Clay sucks in his gut, and I have to fight the urge to tell him to relax. I grab hold of his hand, reminding him I'm here too. We're a unit, no matter what.

"Hey," Roan murmurs, her rubber clogs squeaking with every step she makes towards us.

"Hey, sugar," Clay says, his voice low and gentle like he might scare her.

Am I vibrating? It feels like I am, with every fibre of my being at war with each other. I want to make demands I don't really have a right to, force her to tell me what the problem is right now, right here in front of the whole damn town. We can't help or fix it if we don't know.

More than anything, though, I want to hug her. There is a grey colour to her skin. Some sickly exhaustion haunts her eyes as she looks at both of us. I can barely smell her at all, just a faded berry scent that doesn't seem right. My hand twitches in Clay's as I fight the urge to comfort our Omega.

What in the hell's bells is going on with her?

"Do you mind if we talk somewhere private?" she asks.

"'Course not," I say without a single thought going through my big, stupid head. "You lead the way."

Chapter Nineteen

Clay

MITCH'S GUT REACTIONS AND his impulsivity are the reason for half the messes we get into, at least. He's quick, smart as a fucking whip, but he doesn't always process the words coming outta his mouth until we're tromping through puddles, climbing up the fire escape of the Cove Arts Centre in the dark. We let Roan walk us all the way here in the rain, and now Mitch is lifting her bicycle up the final creaking steps while I pray we don't all fucking slip and die.

Our Omega.

My heart cracks a little more every time I think those words. Is she really ours still? A week ago, I was doing everything I could to stomp down every possessive desire I had. It was important to me she didn't feel stuck, or worse, like we were trapping her with us. She's young and has a whole fucking career and life outside of this town.

Roan doesn't need us, not the way we need her.

She unlocks the door and we all hustle inside.

Woah. I'll be damned. This is a whole-ass apartment.

An empty, sad-looking one that smells of fresh paint and rotten fruit. But I see it. There's a faded, stained rug thrown across the floor. By the kitchen, there's a kettle and one mug that looks suspiciously like the ones Ted uses. Scattered around the place are pages of sketch paper, some with sketches, and others that have been folded into tiny origami shapes. In one corner of the room, a wire is wrapped around two pipes, and it's got clothes draped over it.

Has she been living here for a few days?

"If you'd like, the toilet is there and functioning." She points to the opposite corner of the room. "Do you want a cuppa?"

Mitch nods, shucking off his rain jacket, and I do the same. Next to the door are three pegs. They're old, and the fixtures have been painted over many times, but I can't stop the sentimental part of me noticing the number. I let out a sigh and hang up our jackets.

Our footsteps creak and echo as we walk around this massive, cavernous room. This has just been abandoned here for decades. What Mitch and I would have given to be able to buy this building. We've never even thought about a bigger apartment, but damn, does this make our place feel cramped.

The kettle pops and Roan pours one ceramic mug, then a paper cup. She presents each of us with one, letting us choose. It doesn't smell like the fancy tea I got ordered for her after that first day we met. It smells like a cup of hot, dark water. Mitch takes the ceramic one, leaving me the paper one. It's definitely been reused multiple times, rinsed, and dried out.

But I don't miss my handwriting scrawled across the side.

"Lumzag mentioned you haven't been 'round much," I start. "You staying here?"

She clears her throat. "I had to end my stay, but I asked Connie not to tell."

"Why?" Mitch asks.

It's unclear what the subject of his question is. His tone has an edge of desperation and hurt to it, like he's struggling to hold back tears. It's been a week. Maybe for young people or humans, not talking to someone for a week is normal after you've had only one date.

But for us, for me, it's been a week of aching. Not just for myself, but not being able to console our Beta every time he'd leave the café and come home, still not sure what was going on. I'm an Alpha Wolven, and my job is to keep my pack together, comfortable, and content. We work best as a unit. I can't do that if we're crumbling to pieces.

"Why haven't you come round or answered us when we came knockin'?" Mitch clarifies, words shaking.

Roan can't look either of us in the eye, and I'm further reminded of our age difference, and just how little we actually know one another. Mitch and I have had a whole lifetime together, all our firsts were together. There isn't anything we haven't seen the other do.

But Roan doesn't know us at that level. She doesn't have that trust in us yet. Whatever has been keeping her away has been eating at her soul, if her body language and scent are anything to go by. She sniffles, hugging one arm to herself as she pushes hair away from her face.

"We've been really worried about you, sugar," I say as softly as possible. "We just want to make sure you're okay, taking care of yourself. It's been a helluva week not knowing."

She chokes on a little sob, but steps back when we step forward. Mitch makes an involuntary sound in the back of his throat, and his ears flatten in submission. If I thought my heart was cracking before, it's collapsing like a soufflé now. All the air leaves my body at her unspoken rejection.

"My mum, uh, disowned me last week. The afternoon after our date."

Shit.

Even for the average person, being cut off is awful. I know Roan says she doesn't care about the whole royalty thing, but that's been her whole life. Does she even know how this is going to affect that side of her life?

"She also told me she's essentially been buying my placements for all of my career."

That fucking bitch.

To tear down your own child like that? To not only be thrown into the deep end with no safety net thousands of miles from home, but to have your own flesh and blood cut you that deep?

"Roan." Mitch's voice is barely over a whisper.

"It's fine," she says, trying to swallow the words. "I'm fine."

"Don't lie to us, Omega." I look into her watery eyes. The dark irises glitter with unshed tears, and my throat tightens.

"I'm sorry I ignored you both this week," she pushes on. "It's not fair to either of you after you were so wonderful—"

My instincts take over. My hindbrain screams at me that my Omega is in distress and it is my job to fix. Alphas fix problems.

I wrap my arms around her when she chokes on her apology. She's still soggy from the rain, and her body shakes with a chill. Even if I was the one who cut my familial ties, I still yearn for them and miss the idea of what they could have been. Should have been. It's like pulling teeth—even if you know it's got to go, the yank still hurts and so does the empty spot afterwards.

But it heals.

The sense of loss fades away.

"I know what it's like to feel lost in the world," I murmur. "I know what it's like to have bad parents who don't understand how cruel they are being. But family isn't just the people who raise you. It's who you choose to surround yourself with, who you know will be in your corner."

My fingers curl into her hair as Mitch takes the paper cup from my hand and puts both drinks on the counter. He hugs her from behind, blanketing her in his warmth too. His hands slide between our bellies and squeeze her stiff body.

"Let us be your new family, Omega," he whispers.

She nods against us, rubbing her tears into my shirt while she lets it all out.

It takes a moment. Her breathing is unsteady as she forces herself to remain calm. Then the dam finally breaks. Roan's trembling body slumps into our hold and she sobs—great, unholy sounds.

I look at my Beta, and we're both barely holding it together. The sounds that rack through our Omega are heart-wrenching and defeated, unlike anything I have heard before. Do I see his tears fall or do I feel mine dripping down my fur first? I don't know. It doesn't matter when the three of us are letting everything out.

All the times I've wanted to cry this week bubble up out of me and there is nothing to stop them. Mitch rubs his snout against mine in an attempt to comfort me too, and I almost laugh.

I should be the strong one here. But I worry, and I missed our Omega so damn much. One evening spent with us, one night where our bed was full like it's intended to be, and I knew we'd never be the same. Being without her this week has felt like we've had a piece of our lives missing.

Where Mitch reminds me of a sunny afternoon, his warmth and humour filling my heart with joy, Roan is an early morning. She's cooler, a sense of seriousness and possibility radiates from her that calls me to be better than I was the day before. Both of my mates make me want to be more for them.

Roan makes our pack whole.

"Shh, darlin', just take a deep breath for me," Mitch whispers.

And we all do, collectively trying to pull ourselves together enough so we can talk more than cry. He gives us a final squeeze before he steps back to take his glasses off and scrub his eyes clear of tears. I rub my hand up and down Roan's back until she sniffles one final time.

"Shit, I'm so sorry," she grumbles when she pulls back to reveal the mess she's left on the front of my flannel.

"It's fine, sugar," I say. "S'what the laundry machine's for, ain't it?"

"Nothing says *I'm sorry* like snot stains," Mitch laughs wetly, pulling Roan's handkerchief from his pocket.

He doesn't rub it over his nose, thankfully, but he reaches for me and clears my cheeks. Then he turns Roan around and wipes her face clear, snot and all. She doesn't hesitate to tip her face up to receive the care he's offering. That makes the tightness in my chest loosen some, but I still want to know more about what happened this week.

"Is that mine?" she asks, her bottom lip trembling still.

Mitch hesitates, but I give him the exact look I give him every time I see him carrying that thing around. "Yeah, I took it that day you gave me Clay's mug back. I'm sorry, I wasn't thinking with my upstairs brain."

"It's clean," I add, to make sure she doesn't think we're unkempt perverts.

More tears break loose, along with a series of hiccups that hurt even me. Roan snatches the fabric from Mitch to try and stop her crying. She clutches the handkerchief like her life depends on it. She presses the wet cloth to her chest as she looks at our Beta.

"I thought I lost this," she whimpers.

"I'm really sorry, Omega," he says, ears flattening and shoulders hunching.

"We didn't know it mattered so much to you," I explain. "I'd have made him give it back instantly if we—"

"It's not—" she hiccups.

"You don't have to tell us if you don't want to," I whisper. I want to know. If something is important to our Omega, it's important to us, but my instincts are telling me not to push her.

"I'm just being stupid," she says. "I'm sorry for this past week. If you still want to do this courting thing, I promise I'll be better."

"Roan," Mitch whispers, his gaze moving to mine, looking for guidance.

My tongue pushes into the back of my teeth as my lips purse. Nope. No. Absolutely not. I don't want to hear that kind of language from our Omega. It sets off alarm bells. It stirs memories of my mom promising to be a better Beta when her Alpha and Omega would fight.

I don't say a word as I crouch and throw Roan over my shoulder. She squeals, which thankfully hides my grunt when I straighten again and my knees ache a little. I look around for a place to set her down, but I only see a kitchen countertop.

Fuck, this place doesn't even have anything soft. We need to change that first thing tomorrow. Our Omega deserves better than a fucking rug on the floor.

I move to the counter and Mitch rushes ahead. It's only a few steps, but Roan grips the back of my shirt for dear life. I set her down on the counter, a little hard to make a point. Mitch presses the back of his hand into the cabinet edge to keep her from bumping her head.

We crowd her into the counter, trapping her like prey. I place both hands on either side of her hips. Mitch stands on one side, his arm raised so he can keep her head guarded and to lean into her as he follows my lead.

"Don't you dare," I say, voice harsh and assertive. "Don't ever say shit like that about yourself. We are not perfect, we are always trying to be better, but we make mistakes. But we communicate, Omega. You think we've had twenty years of perfection?"

"No," she whispers, twisting the handkerchief in her lap.

"It's a lot of work," Mitch insists. "He's a lot of work, just like me, but it's not the kind of work you hate waking up to on Monday morning. It's getting to wake up every day knowing that no matter what happens, you've accomplished something amazing. It's another day to show your partners and the world that love is real."

"And it starts with being honest, even if that means being vulnerable," I press. "So tell us, why's the handkerchief matter?"

Roan takes a deep breath, and I think she's going to avoid opening up to us. I noticed this tendency a week ago too. She loves to learn about people, dig into what makes them shine so she can portray them in her paintings, but she doesn't want people to see into her.

"It's to remind myself that I need to believe," she says. "That I deserve the success I earn."

"Nothing stupid about that." Mitch covers her hands with his.

"It is, though, because I haven't earned anything. I haven't done anything," she insists, the tears flooding right back to her eyes. "None of it's been me. It's—it's been her. This whole time."

"Your mother wasn't in our coffee shop two weeks ago," I remind her. "She wasn't in that crowd when you talked us through your paintings. She's not the one controlling your wrists when you're sketching a new idea. She isn't the person who cleared out this entire fucking building by herself.

"You can't change the privilege you grew up with, but you can use it to help your community. You are using it to make things better here. You know people, you know what makes art fancy, you know how to do all sorts of shit that I can't do."

"What if it's not enough?" she asks. "What if—"

"Darlin', you can *what if* until you're blue in the face," Mitch cuts in.

"Don't get so lost in your head worrying that you lose sight of what's right in front of you."

"Two very hot Wolvens," Mitch teases.

I roll my eyes, but Roan laughs.

"Oh my gods," she gasps suddenly, her eyes closing. "I handed Mayor Louise those papers you said I needed to print out. She's going to think I'm some kind of sex pest."

Mitch laughs and laughs. This is just great. The mayor knows more about my Omega's sexual desires than I do. But she did the work we asked her to.

"S'fine, sugar," I say anyway. "I'm the one who's going to read about all the fun you want to have."

"Excuse you, *we* are going to read it. And she gets to read ours." Mitch flicks his tail at me.

"What?"

"We did it too," I say. "The plan was for us to have another date and talk about our interests."

"Which we can still do. We'd still like to do that. Just not tonight," Mitch rushes, his words mumbling together as he yawns.

"You wanna sleep in a real bed, or is that rug some sort of penance you wanna keep up?" I ask.

Roan looks rightfully chastised, but glances at the door. This isn't all the progress I wanted to see tonight. It's a start, and I can't complain about that. We've got plenty of time to peel back the layers of our Omega while she realises she is safe to be her truest self with us.

Chapter Twenty

Roan

THE SMELL OF CAKE wakes me up, buttery soft and covered in vanilla icing. I moan into the warm cocoon of blankets and soft fur that surrounds me. This has been the first good sleep I've had in a week. If I just try a little harder, I can get back to that dream I was having about Clay and Mitch.

"Darlin', you keep rubbin' on me like that and we're gonna have a mess to clean up," Mitch grumbles behind me.

"C'mere, Omega," Clay groans. He wraps his arm around me and drags me the short distance across the bed, until I'm plastered to his soft belly. His nose presses into my neck for a long inhale. My fingers curl into the fur that trails down to his hip, but he stops me before I can touch his stomach. "Now, are you ready to apologise?"

Clay takes my wrists and pins them above my head, his grip gentle. My eyebrows scrunch together, and I look over at Mitch as he puts his glasses on. A lazy smirk forms on his lips when he meets my eye.

"I didn't get a taste of you last week, and I've got such a hankering," Mitch says. "Will you let me?"

I bite my bottom lip and nod.

Mitch's tail wags high in the air as he crawls between my legs. He spreads me open, kissing down my thighs until he reaches my panties. My sleepy eyes follow his movements and he drags my underwear down painfully slowly. Clay presses a kiss into my neck, and I turn my head to him.

"Keep your eyes on our pretty Beta," he murmurs, angling my chin down just as Mitch tucks the band of his boxers under his balls. His dick is hard and dripping already.

He's a gorgeous sight, but...

"I want you too," I say.

I think I see something cross his face. Is it worry? I'm not sure, but Clay shouldn't have a single concern in the world. I want him to be happy and relaxed.

Mitch watches our interaction, but he doesn't say anything.

"Now ain't about me, Omega. It's about you, and soaking our bed with your cum. That's all I'm thinking about right now. All I want. Is that good for you?"

"Yes." The *but* never makes it past my lips.

Mitch dives for my core, his mouth eager to drink me in. My breath hitches as his tongue flicks across my clit. I want to push him down harder, grind on his tongue and teeth, but Clay keeps my wrists held above my head.

"How's he doing, sugar?"

I moan, back arching to push his mouth harder against me. "Yes, that feels good, so good, Beta."

Mitch's claws dig into my hips. His tail wags hard when I compliment him, ass shaking with his excitement. I lick my lips, trying to decide if the words that come to my head are sexy or not. Is it hot to sound like I'm praising someone's work if that work is eating my pussy like it's dessert?

"Keep talking to him," Clay instructs me, his hand moving to massage my breast.

"Oh, fuck," I gasp when his tongue spears into me. "Yes, yes, Beta, fuck your tongue into me. Such a good boy."

At my words, Mitch moans. His body drops to the mattress, and he starts to roll his hips with every thrust of his long tongue. My mouth opens and all the praise, all the encouragement, all the begging I can muster falls from my lips. Every fibre of my being is ready to burst with my need.

Clay presses his muzzle into my neck just as he pinches my nipple. My back comes off the bed as stars burst behind my eyes.

"I'm coming," I screech when neither of them let up.

My pussy clenches hard and fast as Mitch licks my folds, continuing to tease my clit. He hasn't stopped grinding against the bed. I've finished, why aren't we changing positions?

"We're gonna need at least six more, Omega," Clay whispers into my ear. "You were gone so long, we need to make up for all those nights we spent worrying about you."

"Please, Roan," Mitch says, pressing desperate kisses against my flushed skin. "Never want to stop licking your pussy."

I look between my two Wolven. Their eyes are desperate for my pleasure, pleading for me to grant them more of my body. I sink into the pillows and relax.

"I'm all yours."

Is this what I thought it would feel like? The weight of my mother's expectation has been lifted off my shoulder at last, and her all-seeing eyes have finally left me. I don't need to think about her opinion. I don't need to invite her to shows, if I ever land one again.

I simply don't need her.

And yet.

Almost every choice I've made since that phone call, I've doubted. Nothing feels right. I can't trust any decision I make, and I'm constantly looking to Clay and Mitch for some kind of approval, even when they've got no idea what I'm asking about. They are the only choice I've made that I trust.

I've slowly been sharing what my life was like. The opulence that mixed with the constant loneliness and disapproval, stories about realising how deep my family's name protected me and why I came here in the first place.

"What's this tattoo of?" Clay asks one afternoon as we sit on my newly thrifted futon. His claw traces the shape, and a little zip of pleasure shoots through me.

"It's a sprite from an animated movie I loved as a kid." I smile a little. "I haven't watched it in ages."

"We should do a movie night then," Mitch says instantly, ears perking up. "Oh, we can make popcorn balls, and..."

If I could throw open the balcony windows of the Cove Art Centre and profess my love for Clay and Mitch into the street, I would. They are patient with me, listen to my worries without trying to slap on a quick fix, and more importantly, they just accept me as I am.

But screaming at the top of my lungs is not professional, and that certainly isn't appropriate behaviour in front of a decent-sized group of art students. Barnaby has let me borrow several chairs he had stored in the back of the bookstore, and I found a few decent plinths in the first floor storage of the Arts Centre, so the makeshift classroom I set up looks convincing.

"This is a great first crowd," Louise whispers to me.

It's strange seeing the mayor dressed more casual in jeans and a fuzzy jumper. She's got an apron tied around her waist to protect her clothes, but she looks almost mumsy now. It's cute in a weird way.

"Thank you," I say, my smile shaky.

Yeah, it is a great crowd. It's so great and wonderful. Not at all distressing to see so many Hallow's Cove residents in a building that has become my safe haven. For a community that seems so tightly knit together, it's not often you see them out and about rather than working. My life hasn't been hard, I've not had what the world considers a "real" job, but I feel like the community here works too hard and doesn't give themselves a lot of leisure. Shops are open almost every day, quite a few with long hours to accommodate the night-dwelling monsters.

This is something I can provide, easy and safe and laid back. There is no judgment here, and it's short enough that you don't need to worry about closing your business for too long to give yourself something rather than giving to others.

It's a good project, to start.

So why do I feel like there is another shoe just about to drop?

Everyone chats and mingles while we wait for any stragglers and the model to arrive. I've arranged the first floor to be private, but I'm also heavily relying on the afternoon sun bringing in some of the pale lights of autumn. It'll create gorgeous shadows on the model.

Who should have been here by now.

The model, Mal, came highly recommended. When I called around at the art schools in Stonebridge, everyone said they used the same Demon shapeshifter for their classes. One charity art centre was kind enough to give me their number, and they were gracious enough to squeeze us in on a Saturday afternoon. I can't wait to meet them face-to-face.

Hopefully.

As the clock rolls over to our start time, people begin to take their seats, and I have no choice. I excuse myself and head upstairs, where I have my laptop plugged in on an ancient dial-up line. It takes an age and half to get my mailbox to load, but when it finally does, I see an email from Mal.

To: roan@coveartcenter.com
From: malmal666@dmail.com
Re: Life Model Request
Hey,
I won't be able to make it today. My agency double booked me with a magazine gig and I can't back out.
Sorry,
Mal

Do I just jump out the window now? Is this floor even high enough? This is my chance to prove that I'm not a scammer, and now I have no model. Everyone is just going to think I pocketed the money. They're going to hate me.

"Roan?" Clay's voice makes me jump.

I gave the lads a key to the back loft door a few days ago, when I got tired of asking them to come over in the afternoons. Now, after the café closes, they tidy up and come sit with me while I work before we go back to their apartment for the evening.

Clay sniffs a little, and concern clouds his features. It's a look I've grown to know very well. He's always so worried about everything, and I'm coming to realise there is very little I wouldn't do to make him feel better.

"Isn't your class about to start?" he asks.

"Yes," I answer, panic rising. "But I don't have a model for my life drawing class. What are they going to draw? Clear air? The white walls?"

He sets a bag of pastries down on the counter and comes to where I'm hunched over the futon on the floor. I probably look crazy. My thoughts are spiralling from worst-case scenario to even worse scenario. This is awful.

"Sugar." Clay places a warm hand on my back. "It's all gonna be okay. Take a deep breath."

"I can't," I stutter, hands trembling while it feels like the carefully constructed plan I had crumbles to pieces. "Everyone is waiting for me, and I can't let them down."

He closes my laptop and sits down. Rather than letting me up, Clay arranges me between his legs so I'm kneeling between them. His thighs are spread wide and his belly spills into the space between them, and really any other time, this would be hot as hell.

He grips my chin to tear my eyes away from his torso, and away from all the ways I could pleasure him if I weren't about to be run out of town for being a grifter.

"Omega," he grunts, using that private name that's wormed its way right into my brain and turned me to mush for these Wolven. "Do you need support or a fix?"

"Fix," I rush out. "I can't go down there without a model."

"Mitch and I can find someone if you give us thirty minutes," he says calmly, like it's that easy.

"No," I insist. "I need someone now, please. Mitch can't sit still for that long. He won't hold the poses."

I know what I'm implying. He needs to be my model. Nobody else is here. I can't do it myself, because I need to instruct the class. This isn't a fully nude class, but it's still a lot to ask. Clay hasn't even let me see him fully naked yet. The smell of overbaked pastries tickles my nose when I lean into his grip.

"Roan, sugar, nobody wants to draw some fat old Wolven," he murmurs.

"I do," I say, placing my hands on his thick thighs. "I have, over and over again, because you're beautiful. Your body is perfect, Clay. I know it's a lot to ask for you to sit still for a few hours, but nobody is going to think less of you because of how you look. If anything, I'm going to have to beat people off with sticks."

He rolls his eyes like what I'm saying is absurd, but I know it's true. Clay is beautiful. Every curve of his body makes my blood run hot. He's anxious about his weight, I understand that. But it doesn't make me want him less. I want to worship him. If he and Mitch weren't mated, I don't think either of them would be struggling to find other people to be their mates. He just needs to see himself how I see him, how Mitch sees him.

Our mate is gloriously handsome.

"I wouldn't ask if I didn't think you were perfect."

Clay takes a deep breath, but then concedes. "Just for you, Omega."

I grab him by the shirt and pull him down to kiss me. He doesn't hesitate to return my affection, nibbling on my bottom lip so he can deepen it. His claws pinch at my chin, angling me better for his tongue to tease mine.

"Okay, there is a robe in the toilet. Leave your pants on. Come down in a few minutes." I squeeze his thigh. "Thank you so much."

I run down stairs and get the group set up, warming them up by explaining the situation with the model as best I can. My voice shakes more than it did during my first critique. Everyone blinks as if the concept of seeing Clay nearly nude is just another Tuesday.

He comes down stairs a moment later topless. It wasn't what I was expecting, but I don't hate the vision. The white sheet I was going to drape him in to cover his underwear won't be necessary, which is maybe for the better. His jeans should create stronger, more simple folds with higher contrast.

I get Clay situated, placing a glass of water next to his chair and doing my best not to stare. I've seen glimpses of him in the shower or when he's rolling out of bed, but it's always pretty dark. My chest tightens when I think about the amount of sex I've had, but not seen my partner.

He shouldn't feel anything but attractive and sexy and wanted when he's with me and Mitch. His thick fur is soft, the fat that pads his stomach and chest is generous. Clay is beautifully full of life, and his body shows that.

"We'll hold this pose for fifteen minutes and then move to another," I announce, starting the timer on my phone.

"Damn," Bula whispers when I slowly meander around her station. "I need to find a man like that. One of those big boys."

A smile creeps up my face as I see the progress of everyone's sketches. A few times, I remind them not to focus so hard on his face or hands, but rather his full form. For the most part, everyone seems to be having fun blocking shapes.

"Clay, this how you expected to spend your Saturday?" Louise asks.

"Fuck no," he grumbles, trying not to move from his lounging position.

"I'm having the time of my life," Maisie says. "Can I sign Barnaby up for next month?"

The room giggles, and I almost wonder if that could be a thing. The monsters around town posing for the centre art classes seem like a great way to normalise everyone as regular beings, drop any perceptions we have of each other and bare our souls.

Near the final pose, Mitch sneaks in. He makes eye contact with me, eyebrows raised as he looks from me to his mate.

"What kinda spell you put on him, darlin'?"

"It's a long story," I whisper.

I lean into Mitch's side, smelling his sweet warmth and freshly shampooed fur. If I weren't cried out for the day, I'd cry again for how lucky I feel. He slides an arm around my waist while we stare at Clay. We've gone through a lot of poses today, sheets and sheets of paper are scattered across the floor. He must be exhausted, but he seems almost...content.

My alarm goes off a final time, and that's it. Our first class is done. People mingle for only a few minutes to help tidy up. Maisie and Bula both congratulate me on a great first class, and I struggle to accept it. This could have been a disaster. Without Clay, it would have been.

"It's all him," I deflect. "Clay saved my ass."

"It's what mates do," Bula says.

"Barnaby is my rock," Maisie agrees.

Mayor Louise also takes a moment to express her excitement about the success of the class. I promise to come and see her on Monday to return the money we didn't use to pay the model, but she insists I give it to Clay for being so professional while everyone drooled over him.

"But do come and see me, I want to talk about extending your residency," she says, waving as she leaves the Arts Centre.

My jaw drops. She wants me on longer? I swallow back my shock the best I can as blood rushes to my face. I can't believe it. One little afternoon class, without the centre even completed, is all she needed to see to want me to stay longer?

That can't be how this works, right?

In less time than it took to set up the hors d'oeuvres, the gallery is empty. I'm lost in a blur, trying so hard to get everything sorted that I don't even have the brain power to speak more than a few words. Mitch munches on the final carrot baton while I lock up the storage room. We stare at each other in silence for a few moments before he speaks.

"Whatcha thinkin', darling?"

"About what?" I blink.

"About today, the class, our Alpha?"

"Today was stressful, but really good," I admit. "The mayor wants me to stay here a bit longer."

Mitch wraps me up in the tightest spine-cracking hug of my life. His tail wags so hard it shakes us both, and I can't help but laugh. He kisses all over my face, practically licking me. My heart feels so light, so at ease all of a sudden, that I can barely keep the happy tears at bay.

"You know who else wants you to stay?" he asks.

"Connie?"

"No. Well, probably, but me and Clay, Omega. Please say you'll stay?" He stares down at me with the biggest puppy dog eyes I have ever seen. The sincerity warms me, lightens all the weight of the world until I'm floating on a cloud.

"There isn't anywhere else I want to be."

"Shit," he gasps. "We need to tell Alpha."

"Do you think he's okay? He ran up to the loft really fast afterwards. Do you think he's upset with me?"

"I can tell ya right now he was not." He smiles, guiding me upstairs. "One, he smelled divine when I came downstairs, and two, it's good to normalise bigger bodies. He thinks I want the beefy football player he was when we were seventeen, but I want this Clay more than ever."

"I like him this way, too," I say with a sigh, wishing I'd had the chance to pick up my pencil for a sketch during the class.

"Then let's go show him."

Chapter Twenty-One

Clay

THE MOMENT ROAN SAYS that's all the time we have, I bolt. I take the stairs two at a time until I'm left standing in the empty quiet of the loft. There was something different about this, about watching people I've known for years study me.

If it weren't for the occasional comment or question, you'd have thought they'd never laid eyes on me before. I've never felt so seen, yet unfamiliar in town. Even when we first stopped over here, the folks treated us like family. Maybe they could sense something neither Mitch or I could, but they've always accepted us like we belonged here.

This afternoon felt so different. I feel different. My paws shake as I grip the railing on the fire escape, sucking in the cool autumn air.

I didn't just feel like another townie this afternoon, but like a monster who deserves the spotlight for simply being themselves. I couldn't hide away in the bakery or put on an apron. My body was out for them to witness, and I survived.

Worse yet, I heard their appreciation for my body type, their desire as they stared at me between position changes. They wanted me, old and frowning and overweight, and I think I liked it. Why would I like that? I hate being stared at, and it wasn't even my mates who were doing the looking.

Though when Mitch came down the stairs, it became nearly impossible to keep my dick sheathed. Roan had been busy, so her addictive scent was tamped down. Our Beta waltzed in and both of us just started blowing off pheromones like we hadn't fucked in a week.

Whether the audience noticed or not, it wasn't professional of me. It's fucked up enough that this had me feeling all sorts of ways it shouldn't. I can't let Roan and Mitch see me all hot and bothered over this.

I push off the railing, kicking the door closed behind me. A shower would clear my thoughts.

The old faucet creaks to life, and I strip quickly, stepping under the water before it's even warmed up. The shiver down my spine to the tip of my tail doesn't do a damn thing for my leaking dick. My shaft throbs with heat and need. I just need a little release, to take off the edge and calm my thoughts.

I wrap my paw around it and start lazily stroking as my fur absorbs the water. It'd feel better buried in my Omega, feeling her tight pussy mould to me. We've been working on stretching her, playing with her dildo so her muscles are nice and flexible. She begs for my cock every time, for me to push her past the limits just so she can have my knot.

As sweet as those words are, I've always held back. I don't want to hurt her, but on a subconscious level, I'm worried if she sees all of me, it won't live up to her expectations. Today has proven me wrong to some degree. She smelled so fucking divine all afternoon, the blush on her cheeks all the rosier when she looked at me.

"Well now," Mitch announces, smug as all get out.

I turn my head quickly, heat flooding to my cheeks even as I keep fisting my dick. My hindbrain is urging me to keep going, to get out of the shower and fuck my mates into the floorboards. Roan's eyes are glued to my movements, biting her bottom lip as she watches me jerk off. It makes me feel proud, seeing her hunger for me is real. It's probably always been real and right in front of my face, but I've been fucking stupid.

Not anymore.

"Get in here," I growl.

Their scents deepen, clinging to the steam of the shower. Mitch is quicker, rushing in with his socks still on. He's ridiculous, but he's ours. His hard dick rubs against mine as we kiss. It's messy and desperate, his claws digging into me while he rubs against me.

Roan slides in next us in the tight cubicle. She hesitates for a moment, like she's not sure if she's allowed to interrupt us. I grunt, breaking one kiss just so I can pull our Omega into the huddle with another kiss. Her soft skin is flushed red and her tattoos saturated from the water when I take hold of her. As I lean sideways to kiss her, Mitch teases my nipple. Pleasure shoots through me.

She moans as our tongues tangle. Her hot body is pressed against mine without any reservation. When her finger slides over my belly, I freeze, but I don't stop her. She caresses me, holds me like I held her that first night. She wants me as I am, not a version of me that is twenty years younger.

She moves lower until she wraps her hand around my hard shaft. Those little fingers can't even touch, but it feels like she fucking swallowed me whole. My body jerks hard in her gentle grasp.

"Alpha," Mitch rumbles. "You're so fucking gorgeous."

Roan hums along in agreement, pulling back from our kiss to look at me. Her grin is bright enough to light up a stadium.

"Mm-hmm, and you were a natural model. Practically made to be rendered in every lighting," she agrees.

"Y'all just wanna keep me buttered up, don't ya?" I'll agree I look alright, but I know they must be laying it on thick for me. Right?

"You looked so good up there, Clay, and you were good. Like you were basking in all those eyes on you." My heart stalls in my chest at how obvious I was. Mitch continues, "That makes us happy, seeing you get out of your head, realising what a fine Wolven you are."

"Let us show you, Clay, please," she says, playing with my cock while her bottom lip pops out. Gods damn it all.

"How you gonna do that, Omega?" I grunt when her grip tightens. Mitch massages the base of my tail, and I think I might come as the pleasure pulses faster through my veins.

They make eye contact quickly before both of them drop to their knees in front of me. Mitch adjusts our Omega to make sure she's at the perfect angle to suck my cock while he moves a bit lower.

"Beta, what do you love about your Alpha?" Roan asks.

Mitch hums and presses his snout into my balls before he answers. "Where do I start? His soft cheeks, how much I love to steal kisses when we're at work?"

"That's so sweet." Her tone is sincere, even with her mouth so close to my dick.

"What did you expect me to say? That I love when his big, heavy balls slap against my dick when he's taking me from behind?"

"Yes," I grunt.

"I mean, I like it when yours slap against my clit. And Clay's are just—"

Roan cups my balls, hefting them in her hands instead of completing her sentence. That's enough talking. If we don't stop messing around, I'm going to nut over something stupid rather than my mates sucking my dick. I take hold of each of them, pulling them back to look up at me.

"You want to show me how hot my body makes you, you're going to put those mouths to work. If you want a breather or you want to stop, tap my belly twice."

Mitch's eyes roll back slightly, a fluttering of his eyelashes telling me just how fucking ready he is for this. Roan gets that determined look on her face like I've seen a dozen times now. My nails scrape against their scalps gently as I guide them to the tip of my cock.

"Worship your Alpha's dick."

Their lips slide down either side of my shaft, from tip to knot. Mitch's teeth are teasing while Roan drags her tongue across my sensitive skin. I watch them, unable to tear my eyes away. The curve of my stomach may obstruct the view, but that's just a part of me. I don't feel anything but pleasure rippling through my fur as I watch my pack.

Roan moves her head, swallowing my tip and sucking.

"Fuck, that's it, Omega," I moan, and it echoes off the tile.

Mitch takes his chance. He licks down to my knot and sucks one side of it into his mouth. My hips buck, thrusting into the back of Roan's mouth. Her moan vibrates down my cock and lights a fire in my balls.

"Beta, lower."

I can barely get the words out. This is going to end very quickly, but I want it to be big. I want my life to flash before my damn eyes and see my pack old, grey, and well-fucked.

Eager for it, Mitch moves to my sack. He licks between my balls before he sucks one into his mouth, alternating between the two like it's a luxurious treat he wants to savour. I thrust as much as I dare into Roan's hot mouth. One of her hands curls into the wet fur of my thigh while the other moves between her spread legs.

"Hands up, Omega. You do a good job taking your Alpha's cum, then you can get yours."

Her hand flies up to my knot. One squeeze and I'm a goner. There's no warning as my body draws in tight and everything I've got shoots out of me through my dick. Stars sparkle behind my eyes as I watch my Omega swallow my release.

Mitch lets me go as my body relaxes, but Roan keeps suckling at the tip like more cum is going to squirt out of me if she massages my knot right. And maybe it will. It's still half-inflated.

But our Beta is the one to pull her off. He kisses Roan hungrily, tongue burying into her mouth to get a taste of me. They moan together, lost in a desperate haze that I could watch for eternity.

I turn off the shower just as Mitch tugs Roan into his lap.

"Does my cum taste good on her tongue?"

"Yes, Alpha," Mitch groans as our Omega impales herself on his cock. "Fuck, I'll never get used to how good you feel, darlin'."

"Shit, condom." I start to leave as a rush of anxiety hits me, but Roan yanks on my tail.

"I want to be right here with you two, forever," she says, urgently. "I trust you, I trust us. No barriers."

"You have us, Omega," I promise, and I mean it. I want her here with us forever and I know Mitch feels the same. We're a pack.

Roan fucks herself hard and fast. Mitch's claws dig into her hips. Her tits bounce in his face, and I swear his eyes are gonna be crossed forever.

I stoke my half-hard cock as they fuck on the shower floor. Their pleasure bounces off each tile like a song, coordinated and perfect. Everything smells like sex and blueberry pie.

Roan orgasms with a silent scream, her mouth open and practically begging for more cum. She looks up at me, and I set my cock on her tongue again. Mitch grinds her down onto his pelvis and he shakes with his release.

One tiny spurt comes out of me as a shiver rakes through me.

"Feed it to him," I murmur.

Her mouth is still open, cum on her tongue as she presents it to our Beta. Mitch licks into her. He takes what she's offering and swallows. They sigh, relaxing into each other when their needs are satisfied for now.

"Clay, you're too tall," Roan whines.

"I'm not kneeling on the tile, Omega."

Both of them pout at me, like kids begging for an ice cream dinner.

I step out of the shower quickly and grab the stack of hand towels Mitch uses for his skincare routine. He scoots them over enough for his back to rest against the wall. I fold a couple towels and place them under each of Roan's knees before I get a larger towel for me. Folding it into a good kneeling pad, I lower myself down to their level.

Roan leans over and kisses me. Her lips are tinged with the taste of me still, and a possessive pride fills my chest. Mitch makes my heart want to burst when he kisses me next. My pack is all mine to take care of, to cherish, to love. And they want to do the same for me.

I couldn't be happier than I am right now.

Chapter Twenty-Two

Mitch

MORNING LIGHT BREAKS THROUGH the curtains, and I pull the covers up over my head to hide. It's too early. It's too cold. I'm too sore.

I don't know where Roan gets her energy, but she isn't sharing. We've spent all of October and the first two weeks of November building and moving furniture around at the Arts Centre. It took one minor trip to the emergency room after she sprained her wrist for Clay to put a full stop on her insistence she can do it all herself. Obviously, there was a bit of argument about that, but Clay was the voice of reason. A part of being independent is knowing when to lean on your supports and your community. It's something we are still working on with her.

We're deep in the offseason until after the holidays, so that means we're closing up the café at noon every day and going to work at the centre with Roan.

I'm not meant for physical labour. I'm an old, old wooden ship. I deserve to be polished off regularly and paraded around while we talk about my former glory as a seafaring vessel. Now I'm being taken down to the docks and forced to haul two-by-fours up stairs.

My back twinges just thinking about having to carry the giant armchairs Barnaby is donating up to the first floor. Why does the first floor have to be where people lounge? Why can't they do that on the ground floor?

Clay hasn't complained once about the heavy lifting. The fact that he passes out the moment his head hits the pillow says it all, though. He's feeling as run down as I am. We've taken to having lunch in the café just so we can all eat one meal together before we are running off to do our own things, or before we fall asleep at seven in the evening like some kind of geriatric wizards.

It will all be over in a couple of weeks, with the Cove Arts Centre's official opening and show. We are proud of our Omega and all the work she's putting in to make this special for the people in town. Every morning, she runs off to interview someone else and spend time with them while they work. She wants to fill the first floor with portraits of the unsung heroes in our community.

Barnaby, Andri, Connie, and Naia have offered to share art from their collections and vintage pieces about the town to display on the ground floor. The mayor's office has also donated a few older documents about the town. Roan's hope is that it draws tourists in for the history, and then she can lure them upstairs with modern art and really push people to learn about Hallow's Cove, rather than just remember we exist for a week every summer.

It feels like things are finally settling into place. Our pack is complete and we are growing. I see it in all of us, and I couldn't be more proud of our Omega for joining and accepting us.

Clearly, I am more awake than I want to be. Maybe if I get up now, I can make Roan a tea before she runs off. Can you put foamed milk in tea? Does that add anything fun to it? I feel like I'm being denied my chance to show off every day when all she wants with her drink of choice is cold milk.

A splash of ice-cold milk.

There is nothing fun about that. No foam art. No fun flavours meddling together with freshly ground coffee. It's just leaves with hot water.

Maybe that's where she gets the energy?

I shove my feet into my slippers and look at the alarm clock on Clay's side of the bed.

9:23

Nine?

Shit. Fuck. Why would they let me sleep? Clay can't work the espresso machine. He can just barely operate the drip filters. Fuck, fuck, fuck.

My foot slams into Roan's suitcase and I double over. She doesn't have a lot of stuff. Her whole life was packed up into these two suitcases, but shit. Our apartment isn't really big enough for the three of us. Maybe once the centre opens, we can hunt for a bigger place, somewhere that suits all of us.

I pull a sweater over my head while trying to write that thought on a Post-It note before I run down the front stairs to the shop.

"Welcome," Roan says with a giggle from behind the counter. She's wearing a tiny little apron cinched at her waist and one of my old t-shirts that's so tight I can see the outline of her bra.

Damn it. She has no right to be so damn sexy when I'm late.

I point my finger right at her as I step up to the counter. "Darlin', you got a lotta nerve stealing my apron."

"We don't serve that here." She smiles. "Just lattes and looks."

"We don't recommend the lattes," Jeremy says from where he's sitting with someone new.

I do a double-take at the new person in town, but I don't get a chance to ask their name before Roan pesters me for my coffee order.

"I'll make it," I say, rounding the corner. "You watch, I'm not risking my first cup of the day."

"So what's your drink?" she asks, moving to sit on my stool.

"It's a double macchiato with whipped cream."

"Does the whipped cream make it more fun?"

"I like it better than adding sugar." I smile, pushing the portafilter under the coffee grinder until I get the weight I'm looking for with this blend.

Roan sits quietly while I make my coffee until I'm knocking the puck out. She hops off the stool and goes for the small fridge with the glass front under the counter.

I'm not the least bit ashamed to say I stare at her ass when she's bent over.

She gives the whipped cream canister to me, but I slide my cup to her.

"You're the one wearing the apron."

There's a gleam in her eyes when she gives the can a shake and turns it upside down over my drink. Clay said it was a silly investment to get the fancy professional thing when the store-bought cans worked just as well. But our Omega looks downright fucking evil when she pulls the trigger and cream explodes everywhere.

It covers both of us in cream and hot coffee. Roan squeals as she drops the canister onto the floor, and more cream shoots up at her face. The fluffy white cream arcs with precision up in the air and lands right on her cheek and slides down to her chest.

Clay throws the door to the kitchen open as I'm curled over cackling. He huffs, looking from me to her, and then at whipped cream everywhere.

"You good, sugar?" he asks.

Roan's bottom lip pops out when she sees the true extent of the mess. And yeah, it makes me want to pout, too. This is a disaster.

"I just wanted to do something nice," she groans.

"And you are," Clay answers, grabbing a few washcloths from under the sink. "You're helping him clean up."

"Last time I use that busted can," she grumbles in a grouchy tone that sounds like Clay.

I have to swallow my laughter as we get to cleaning up. It doesn't take long, but I write myself a Post-It note to do a deeper clean this afternoon. The last thing we want is a café that smells like turned milk.

While Roan does a final mop of the floor, we get suddenly slammed with a group of bird-watching tourists. I don't know what's going on, but not only do I get bogged down in making lattes on lattes, Roan steps in to take orders and payment as well. The whole front of the shop is suddenly bursting with people and the echoes of chatter.

When was the last time it was this busy? What happened to the offseason? I can smell the dry cream on my fur, and all I want to do is crawl upstairs and shower. My feet ache from wearing my slippers all morning. We can't even close at noon like we planned. It's four in the afternoon by the time we've got the crowd cleared out and the café cleaned to a respectable standard.

"Omega," I whine, draping myself over her back. "Carry me, I'm dead."

"If you're dead, you don't get the rest of your surprise," she laughs. "It'll just be me and Clay having all the fun."

I groan. "You know I can't be left out."

"Then we've got to liven up," she says with a pat to my hand on her stomach. "Help me grab something from across the street, and then we can have shower sex."

My ears perk up at that, and I suddenly feel rejuvenated. I grab Roan by the hand to get us out of here, not giving a single fuck about ruining my slippers. They're probably already ruined. I'll buy a new pair if it means getting my Omega all wet and slick after our day together.

Roan unlocks the front of the gallery and ushers me in quickly. There are stacks of covered frames and the smell of fresh paint is finally fading away. There is still a lingering smell of sawdust from the work we've been doing, but it's not chemically offensive like the paint.

My stomach grumbles when I catch a whiff of something sweet.

"Did you take a break to eat?" I ask, looking down at my mate. I can't remember if I told her to stop and eat during the day. I saw plenty of pastries and cakes going from the cabinets this morning, but I don't think I saw her take a single bite of anything.

"I'm fine," she says, shoving me towards the stairs. "Let's go."

"Don't make me tell Clay you didn't eat," I threaten.

"He's not going to care," she huffs.

"Oh, you wanna bet?"

We round the stairs on the first floor, and I get a little starstruck looking at the finished painting of my fellow townies. My mate painted these. She's done all this work in such a short period of time, but I can only imagine the lasting effect it's going to have. The paintings are all different, beautiful and special to each person.

"Mitch!" She stomps her foot.

"Geez, so pushy." I smirk, looking from a painting of Gabe back to my Omega. "Desperate for me already, darlin'?"

Her cheeks tint that adorable pink shade that makes my dick hard. It doesn't stop her from grabbing my hand and dragging me toward the ever-growing sweet smell coming from the loft. Did she get some kind of incense or something?

"I asked Clay, and he said you wouldn't mind." Roan's voice takes on a nervous edge as she opens the door to her space.

It's not as blindingly bright as it used to be. I cock my head to the side as I follow her into the room. There are tall wardrobes in the corner, and she's rearranged the furniture and...

Is that our cuck chair?

It's never been used for that, but I heard someone talking about the concept years ago and it was too funny to ignore. Clay mostly uses that chair to put his socks on in the morning, and I always end up throwing my pajama pants on it.

Now though, it's angled next to Roan's futon and our TV is set up opposite it. Roan drags me around, grabbing my hand and taking me around the corner to reveal that our dining table is here now. There is a far corner set up for her art supplies and a desk has been set up, too, so she has a proper space for her laptop.

The sweet smell is cupcakes.

On our bed.

With Clay. Who is naked.

The golden glow of the setting sun lights him like a hedonistic god, and I never want this image to leave my brain. It's so perfect, the way the light makes his grey fur glow. My dick hardens painfully quickly just looking at him.

"Fuck me," Roan breathes. "This is extra."

"You can call me the king of surprises." Clay grins, hard cock laying on his thigh while he licks frosting off a tiny cake.

I look from my Alpha to our mate, clutching my imaginary pearls. Her lips are parted as she stares at him. Never in his life has Clay been one for surprises. If anything, I am the king of surprises. He's stealing my thunder and honestly, I could weep tears of joy right now. He sounds so fucking content with himself.

"There is a warm towel in the microwave for you to wipe off with," he notes casually. "But we're going to get very, very messy."

Chapter Twenty-Three

Clay

MITCH SPRINTS FOR THE towel, throwing off his clothes while he does it. Roan strips right in front of me, her eyes never leaving my dick.

When Roan had found out this floor was zoned to be an apartment, she'd been shy about asking if Mitch and I would want to move in here. Nothing against our studio, but it's small, especially now with the three of us.

It was her idea to make furnishing the apartment a surprise for Mitch, and I jumped at the opportunity. It's not every day I get to plan and be spontaneous at once. Usually, surprises make me break out in hives, but being the surpriser is unexpectedly thrilling.

With the help of Rick and Ted, we made short work of getting the big pieces of furniture up here. Ted grumbled a bit, but I promised him a free weekly pie for a year if he did me a solid. I also may have mentioned to him that he did sort of owe my mate an apology for spreading shitty rumours about her.

Rick was an easy sell, because I paid him. Money talks with that guy, and props to him for it. He's here to run a business, and I respect that. Plus, it was worth it to see Mitch's eyes go wide at all the space. He can spread out when he likes to, or stay up late with Roan if I'm going to bed early.

"Let me, Omega," he says, coming up behind Roan to unhook her bra.

I swallow my last bite of cake watching my Beta run the warm towel over her skin. The tattoos shine when they're damp, and I love seeing her art displayed for us. Roan's body is its own gallery of stretch marks, dimples, and tattoos.

Mitch tosses the rag over his shoulder when he's done. Reaching for one of the cupcakes, he scarfs one down, moaning when he realises the flavour is blueberry and vanilla buttercream.

"It's us," he mumbles around a mouthful.

"Let me taste," Roan demands, pulling his hand to her mouth to lick and suck the crumbs off his fingers.

These two will be the death of me, enjoying the view of them feeding each other my bakes. I move the tray of cupcakes from the edge of the bed to the nightstand, though. As fun as it would be to ruin our sex blanket with icing and cum, I can't trust any of us not to smear cake where it doesn't belong in a fit of passion.

I stroke my cock slowly, watching Mitch smear icing across Roan's neck before licking it clean off. She whimpers, her scent growing sweeter as our mate teases her. My knot throbs with desire. I've had this planned all week, and the satisfaction of it coming together this well makes me harder.

"You two are gonna spoil me," Mitch groans against her throat.

"C'mere, Beta," I say.

He awkwardly moves Roan with him as he falls into bed. Her giggles echo around the high ceilings, and I wonder if her moans will, too. There is plenty of time to learn, but right now I want to hear my Beta say *thank you.*

"What do you say to your Alpha?" I ask.

"It's about fuckin' time," he growls a little as he climbs on top of me.

Not the answer I wanted, but when he kisses me, it takes my breath away. Mitch licks into my mouth, grinding his hips against my belly. My fingers dig into his ass to encourage him, working him faster against me as his pre-cum smears across my fur.

"Gods, you're so fucking hot," he moans into my mouth. "Do you know that, Alpha? Just looking at you makes me go a bit stupid. You smell so good—so good for us."

"Show me, Beta," I challenge him, nipping at his bottom lip. "Show our Omega what I do to you."

His claws dig into my shoulders as he thrusts against me. The bed squeaks with his effort. He closes his eyes tight, but I know he's gonna lose focus if we don't rotate.

"Switch," I pant.

Mitch nods, rolling off of me as we switch our position, lying sideways on the bed to stop the squeaking. He straddles my stomach again, his dick curving to match the roundness of my belly as he slowly drags it through my fur. Roan sits on the edge, her bottom lip caught between her teeth.

"Take these," I say, passing her the packet of wipes I brought over with the groceries. "Don't be afraid to squeeze his tail."

She eagerly takes them, and I get the pleasure of watching it dawn on Mitch exactly what's to happen.

"Damn, is it my fucking birthday?" he teases, rising up a little to present his ass to her.

"No," I laugh. "So you better get to work before I knot our Omega."

Our Beta's knot leaves her a little sore the next day, and I'm terrified of what mine would do without the preparation. We've been working on it when we have the energy, teasing our girl with her Demon dick over and over again while we train her muscles to stretch. Her begging and pleading for my knot plays like a soundtrack in my head every time we practise.

Today, we're going all the way.

Mitch shivers as Roan cleans him up to her liking. His claws dig into my chest in anticipation. I hear her deep breath and watch Mitch's eyes roll back as she starts eating his ass. His sharp inhale blends with the warm vanilla scent coming from him like a mall bath shop.

"Such a pretty Beta," I praise him. "Tell our Omega how you like it."

Mitch is a little too lost already, working his hips to mark me with his pre-cum while our girl teases his asshole. Gods, I'm glad we all did those fucking worksheets. Ours remained pretty much the same, with Mitch including that he wanted to top a bit more and try his hand at taking control.

But learning everything that Roan wanted to try was like Christmas coming early.

"C'mon, sunshine," I encourage when he remains wordless. Truly a feat that I'm gonna have to remember for another time.

"I— Oh, fuck," he grunts. "Yes, just like that Omega. Grab my tail. I like slow licks at first, ones that get faster and faster."

His voice rises in pitch as she does what he says. Her hand lands on my thigh and squeezes as we rock the bed. I'll never get tired of watching my mate, the needy sounds he makes as he chases his orgasm. Mitch's shaft glistens with pre-cum, smearing it across my fur with every stroke. I know he's close, so I dig my claws a little tighter into the meat of his thighs.

"Be a good boy now," I whisper. "Come for your Alpha, mark him up real good. Let everyone know I belong to you, Beta."

"My Alpha," he pants, hips jerking erratically until they stutter to a stop. Cum shoots out of his dick and across my belly and chest. The red tip flexes with his release, and his knot deflates almost instantly when there's nothing clamped around it.

"Roan, please," he whines. "I can't anymore."

There's a loud, smacking kiss before she pops up, wrapping her arms around Mitch. She kisses his shoulder and back while he gasps for air.

"Did I do a good job?" she asks, a sly smile on her face that says she knows the answer.

"The best," he grunts.

Mitch collapses on the bed next to me. He pants, one hand wildly flapping up toward my face as if he's just run up the side of Twilight Peak.

"You two now," he says. "That's my dying wish."

"That so?" I ask.

He nods.

"If he's going to die, I think we ought to follow his wishes, Alpha," Roan says.

Her voice is teasing, but my dick fucking jumps to attention. She doesn't use Mitch's designation often, usually in the heat of the moment or when she's feeling especially bratty.

But me?

I've only ever been Clay to her. I haven't pushed her on it, because I understand humans have co-opted the Wolven's natural hierarchy to be something disgusting. Hearing her say it now is like a dream come true. It sounds so natural coming from her; the way her accent catches on the vowels is so different than anything I've heard before.

I grab her by the waist and yank her body up mine. I don't care that it's smearing more of Mitch's cum into my fur. I need her lips on mine. I need to feel her tongue and I need to smell all that sweetness at the source. Roan makes a noise of surprise, but falls right into me when my hand curls around her neck.

"Mouth," she panics.

"Don't care," I growl, unable to keep the feral edge from my voice before my mouth slams against hers.

She's mine. My Omega.

I lick into her and taste everything she has to offer. Mitch and I have been together a long time, and her tasting like him just makes my knot swell. She moans into our kiss when it seems to click that I don't give a fuck about anything but having her right now.

"You ready, sugar? Going to be a good Omega who takes her Alpha all the way?"

"Yes, please," she answers quickly. "How do you want me?"

"So eager," Mitch hums. "Love that about you."

"Are you comfortable with me behind?" I ask.

Her eyes light up at the suggestion. I know it's not the most romantic position, but my knot is heavy from all the stretching we've been doing without a full release. We're going to be stuck together for a while afterward, and I want to make sure she's comfortable.

Roan crawls into position, dropping to her elbows to present her ass to me. It's perfect. My hindbrain is like a broken record telling me two things and two things only.

Fuck and *love*.

That's all it is with them. I've loved Mitch since we were kids, but my love for Roan is so new. It's fresh and different. It's like topping a cobbler with whipped cream to cut through all that sweetness. I want to eat her up until the whole tray is empty. Just a scoop of the love I have for Mitch and Roan just wouldn't cut it.

My cock slides through her cunt, which is slick with arousal. I smooth my hands over her hips, spreading her ass as I line up with her pussy.

"Deep breath, Omega," I say. "You're going to take everything I give you."

"So pretty like this, Roan," Mitch encourages her. "You were made for us."

I push the slim tip of my cock into her slowly. Her body gives easily, but I hold there, even if it means it feels like my knot is going to explode. My balls ache with the same urge. I want to plow into my Omega, bury myself so deep inside her that she'll be leaking my cum until I can fuck her all over again.

"More, Alpha," she moans, moving to her hands to try and push back into me.

"Who's in charge, sugar?" I grit my teeth.

"You are," she pouts, but I can hear the smile in her voice. "But a girl's got needs. I've been so good with our practising."

"Beta," I signal, mouthing the word *tease.*

I pull out of Roan completely. She whimpers, but I'm more than capable of waiting if it means asserting my position in our pack. I am the Alpha. My role is to be in charge. Mitch reaches over to the tray of cupcakes and swipes a finger through the icing. His face disappears beneath her torso, and her little gasp is enough to tell me he's sucking on her nipples. Her empty pussy clenches as I tap my dick against her.

"Oh, fuck," she groans.

I slide my tip a bit deeper into her and pull out again. It's sweet music listening to her moan and whine while we pleasure her without giving her what she's desperate for. Her pussy squeezes me hard every time I dip into her, trying to keep me inside her. But I don't stop until she's shaking, her juices dripping down onto the blanket. Her cunt easily swallows my shaft, her body relaxed and willing. She's ready for me.

"Who's in charge?" I ask again.

"You."

"Who owns this pussy?"

"You, Alpha," she whimpers. "You do, please, I need you."

My hand slides up her back until I'm grasping her nape. "What's your safe word, sugar?"

"Toast," she confirms quickly.

"Good girl."

I slam forward until my knot is partially buried in her tight pussy. Shit, does that feel good. Her body gives and stretches and holds my dick so fucking well. I pull out to the tip and fuck into her again.

She's slick, her muscles pulsing with need. I groan as I fall into a rhythm, getting lost in the clutch of her cunt. My body tingles as my balls draw in tighter with every wet slap against her clit. I'm running on the edge of oblivion every time our bodies come together.

"Please, please, please," she cries out.

"Come on my dick, Omega."

"I need more."

My fingers curl against her skin, teasing and dangerous. Just a little, just enough. I look at Mitch, at the lazy smile on his face as he watches us. He strokes his cock, but I know he can't come again this soon.

"Beta," I bark. "Give our Omega what she needs."

"Yes, Alpha." He grins.

I don't like that look. I know that look.

Mitch moves down to my thighs, kicking his fucking feet like a teenager. I know the moment his fingers touch Roan's clit, because her pussy has a death grip on my dick. Mitch's other hand cups my balls, massaging and squeezing them like he's trying to fucking milk me.

"I'm gonna knot you, sugar. Hold on tight for me. Want you to make a fucking mess for us." I grunt and groan like I've lost my damned mind.

Maybe I have. Maybe this level of delirium isn't safe. All I know is it drives me wild, watching my Omega shake as I fuck her hard, hearing her pussy slurp every time I fuck into it.

"Show me how it's done, Alpha," Mitch moans. It's exaggerated, pornographic, but shit does it work.

I snap my hips forward hard. Roan shouts as my knot buries itself into her tight cunt. Lightning shoots through my dick as I come. Her body spasms uncontrollably, fluids splashing across my thigh as her orgasm takes her. She collapses forward, and I have no choice but to go with her. Mitch pulls his hands out just in time before we're smooshed together and lying in our mess.

"So proud of you, Omega," I murmur. "Such a pretty girl for us. You did so well."

She hums, curling her finger around one of mine. I press kisses along her cheek and neck for a while, content to lie here in the quiet. Our Beta tries to slip out of bed, but she's not having any of that. I've never seen her move so fast as when she grabs him by the arm.

"Stay," she commands.

"Such a bossy Omega," he chuckles.

"As she should be," I agree, nuzzling into her neck to smell her syrupy goodness.

Mitch rolls us towards the headboard and out of the mess. Fuck, it's a good thing I put that blanket down. The wet patch is massive. He folds up the edge to cover it and lies down facing Roan. She grabs his hand and presses it to her cheek.

"Thank you," she murmurs, her eyes closed.

"For what?"

"For loving me." She sighs, sleep slowly taking over her.

I look at Mitch over her shoulder. His eyes sparkle with tears as he brushes his thumb over her rosy cheek.

"Do you?" I ask quietly.

"'Course I do," he whispers. "Don't you?"

"Is the sky blue?"

He hums, closing his eyes too as a smile curls on his lips. "We're a pack."

"Yeah, we are."

Chapter Twenty-Four

Roan

IT'S TONIGHT. IT'S REALLY happening. Oh gods, I'm going to be sick.

I've spent all day running around. There are so many tiny things that have to be done before a show that I've never considered before. Information cards, those tiny toothpicks for hors d'oeuvres, and oh yeah, the guest list.

Why did I let the mayor convince me this should be an invitation-only opening? We invited basically everyone anyway. Why does it need an invitation? Just because someone says they'll be here doesn't mean they will actually show up. Everyone could mysteriously get food poisoning and have to stay home. Is it better if no one shows up? I'm not sure I could cope with such a poor opening.

"Roan, darlin'?" Mitch grunts. "Is this good?"

I blink.

He and Maisie are holding up the final painting Barnaby has donated to the back wall on the ground floor. It's some landscape in an Impressionist style. Barnaby says it's of Hallow's Cove before the ruffians settled, but if you asked me, it could be literally anywhere. The heavy golden frame is ornate and makes it look like a piece that actually belongs in a museum with a full team of conservators.

"Yes, sorry, that's perfect," I say quickly.

They make quick work of securing the screws into the wall and placing the painting. I slip the postcard-sized information card into the acrylic stand balanced next to it.

"Nice work." Maisie raises her hand for a high five, and I'm more than happy to agree. They have been absolute troopers today helping with the final prep work while Clay has been baking up a storm.

"Okay, you and Barnaby are still good to come by thirty minutes early, right?" I ask.

"For sure," Maisie says. "Everyone's dying to see their portraits."

I nod. "Let's hope nobody tries to run me out of town afterwards."

"Puh-lease." She rolls her eyes. "This is great. Everyone loves a good reason to get dressed up, and you're providing free food. Nothing could go wrong."

I don't tell my friend all the horrible ways in which it absolutely could go wrong. Those are inside thoughts.

"C'mon, darlin'," Mitch cuts in, wiping the sweat from his brow. "We all need to get gussied up and put on our Sunday best."

Maisie gives us a final salute as she walks out the front door. Mitch turns the lock behind her as I wave through the window.

"No more bad thoughts," he announces. "Get that fine ass upstairs and cleaned up."

I put my hands on my hips at his bossy tone. Mitch grins even bigger as he wraps me up in a hug. My shoulders slump into his warmth and sweet scent.

"You got this, Omega," Mitch says. "Everyone is going to love it."

I shake my head as stress tears spring to my eyes.

"And if they don't, we can make Clay beat 'em up."

That does bring a weak smile to my face. Clay would never, but it's fun to think about. There's really nothing else I can do. Everything is hung up, tablecloths and decorations are placed. All that's left to do is shower and wait to open the doors to all of Hallow's Cove.

"If we head up now," Mitch says with a nudge of his hip in the direction of the stairs, "we can shower together and let our Alpha catch us having sexy times."

My body heats at the idea, even as I laugh at the way he's said it.

"Well, I can't say no to that."

Damn.

My Wolven look fit in a suit. Even if their idea of dress shoes are cowboy boots, they look hot as sin. Clay adjusts Mitch's jacket to make sure there are no stray pieces of lint. His dark navy suit has already been pressed to death, and the black shirt underneath is spotless. Unlike Mitch's, which had been covered in hair and dust.

"We don't get dressed up often," he says as an excuse. "'Course it's disgusting."

A trip to the dry cleaners was well in order for it and my own dress. Over the long flight and staying buried in the bottom of my suitcase, the designer garment had been a nightmare when I dug it out three days ago.

Now the structured material lays as it should. It's artistic and timeless. One of the few nice things my mother ever did for me was insisting I get this dress.

"I feel like we don't really need to go downstairs," I say. "We could stay up here, ruin our smart outfits."

"You ain't getting outta this," Clay says. "Bad enough we're runnin' behind because I couldn't say no in the shower."

My tummy flutters thinking about the orgasms they just gave me. I could still go for more—certainly better than facing any crowd downstairs.

"It was a good shower and we got all squeaking clean," Mitch says with a grin.

Clay grunts, herding us to the door. Mitch leads the way, and I'm happy about that. I don't think I could have taken the first step if I wasn't sandwiched between my mates.

On the first floor, Andri has set up a large bar, and Clay has arranged piles of bite-sized pastries for everyone to pick at throughout the night. The building looks gorgeous, so incredibly different from when I first saw the inside. I'd never even believe this place was shuttered for over fifty years.

I take a deep breath as I hear the chatter of the crowd downstairs. Their excited voices and laughter carry in waves. It rises and rises, threatening to overwhelm me and drag me under.

Clay tucks his finger under my chin. I look in his clear blue eyes and the shades of grey in his fur, and I realise he'd never let me sink. Mitch kisses my cheek and takes my hand.

"You got this, Omega. Everyone is going to love it," he assures me.

"And before anyone can say it, we are so unbelievably proud of you," Clay says. He swallows hard, eyes flicking to Mitch before focusing on me again. "We couldn't imagine sharing our life with anyone else but you, sugar."

"We love you so much."

Tears well up behind my eyes when I look at my mates. They love me. My heart swells like a big fucking balloon and bursts with happy confetti.

"I love you, too," I blubber, trying to hold in tears so I don't ruin my makeup.

"Thank gods," Mitch chokes, pulling us in for a hug. "Our pack."

"Our pack," Clay agrees.

"Are you sure we can't go back upstairs?" I ask one final time, only half joking.

My mates laugh, even as they lead me down the wider set of stairs to the ground floor.

It's crammed full of people. They all turn, Mayor Louise rushing up to me. I'm not sure exactly what she says, because my ears are suddenly full of cotton as all eyes land on me.

"...and now for the lady of the hour."

It takes a beat for me to realise I'm that person. My cheeks heat and my palms dampen with nervous sweat. Why does this feel so much bigger than anything I've done before?

"Thank you, everyone," I start, my voice shaking. "I know my presence in Hallow's Cove was a shock, considering no one knew the mayor had posted this job for a resident artist."

There is a scatter of laughter, and I have to swallow to keep the rocks in my stomach at bay.

"But I can't thank you all enough for welcoming me into your community. I know it was a rough start for some of us, but I have never seen a more dedicated group of people. I appreciate you giving me your time and energy, your laughter and your wisdom. It is an honour to share the opening show of the Cove Arts Centre with you."

And that's it. That's all the words I can muster before I awkwardly gesture for people to head upstairs. I stand at the bottom, flanked by Clay and Mitch like they're some kind of security detail. A rush of people move by, some congratulating me while others simply smile.

At the tail end of the group are three older Wolven. One walks with a cane, while others walk on either side of her like both her bodyguards and her dates.

"There's my baby." One grins from ear to ear, quickly breaking away from their pack. They scurry up to Mitch and wrap him in a big hug, despite being closer to my size.

"You came," he says, voice going all soft. "We've missed you so much."

Clay circles his arm around my waist as Mitch hugs the other two Wolven. The one with the cane eyes Clay and then me before breaking out into a grin I know all too well on our Beta. It's teasing and mischievous and clearly genetic.

"Well now, what do we have here?" Her voice is low, with a deep Southern drawl I thought only existed in movies.

"Mom," Mitch says, speaking directly to her. "This is Roan. She's our Omega."

I hold out my hand, but she pulls me into a hug tight enough to crack my back. Unlike Mitch, she smells sort of like nothing—maybe perfume—and that is almost as jarring as the hug. I guess that mates' smelling thing is more real for me than I thought.

"We're so happy to finally meet you," she murmurs. "Mitch sent us the invite, teasing us with a special surprise."

"Sweetheart," a manly voice intones softly, "don't crush the poor girl to death."

"Right, right. You can call me Rosey," she says, pulling back but not letting go of me. "Clay, having a pack suits you."

"Thank you, ma'am," he says.

Mitch introduces me to his dad, John, and his mimi, Trish. They flew all the way up here to see the show tonight because Mitch asked them to. They're excited for an excuse to get away, and so happy to see their son with the pack they dreamed he'd have.

Before they make their way upstairs, I notice how Rosey and Clay shake hands, the whispered *thank you* that's just between them.

I'm not left with long to wonder about that, because it's finally time for us to head upstairs. Both lads kiss my cheek as we reach the top.

"Do your thing, sugar."

I find Barnaby and Maisie first, dressed finely and staring at their opposing portraits. Old and new. Again, I'm pulled into a hug by Maisie when I ask them what they think.

"Extremely well done," Barnaby says. "With the building and with our portraits."

"Just how you remember it?" I ask.

"Better," he says, a gentle smile forming on his lips as he looks at Maisie.

It gets easier walking around and chatting with people from town and posh ski lodge visitors. With fresh snow on the mountain, the winter tourist season has officially started. Gnurl and Bula gush over the finalised portrait of

Connie as she poses next to it for photos. She drags me in for a hug and more photos of us together.

"I can't thank you enough," I tell her between flashes of her husband's Polaroid camera. Her fingers curl into my waist as we hold our pose. "Your kindness and openness mean the world to me."

"That's what family's for," she says simply, hugging me tighter.

It's nearly midnight by the time I've spoken with everyone. There is only one person I haven't talked to all night, and he's been sitting in the corner with a perfect view of his portrait. Ted doesn't move as I approach him, his sport coat wrinkled around his folded arms.

"So what do you think?" I ask, standing next to his chair to see the tall painting.

He makes a *harrumph* noise.

I didn't think it was that bad. It depicts him, dour expression on his face as he stands above a faceless, gossiping crowd. He's holding an order pad from the diner, a pen tucked behind his ear, and he takes note of everyone and everything.

"Makes me look like a bad guy," he finally says.

"I don't know," I say. "I see a monster who sees all, hears all, and protects all."

"Calling me a gossip now?"

"Yes and no." I shrug. "You told people I was trouble when I wasn't, but I also know from all the interviews, people around here take your word seriously. They trust you to whittle out the truth and give it to them straight."

Ted grumbles something, but then offers me his hand to shake. I'm happy to take that for the truce that it is. Something about Ted's response puts me at ease. I didn't magically change his mind to like me, and I'm happy for that.

I walk back around the gallery, trying to make my way to the refreshment table at long last when I do a double-take at the stairwell.

Coming up the stairs is a couple. One is an Elf with sage green skin and silken hair, clearly from a royal family based on the pattern of their robes.

And next to them stands Donovan.

I stop dead in my tracks when we make eye contact. I'm sure he looks the same as he did last time I saw him, but I'm still categorising his features all the same. His hairline has recessed slightly, but his hair is still dark. He's dressed in a hand-stitched suit, pocket square firmly displaying the Farrador colours.

He looks very much like the marquis he was born to be.

"Rowey," he says with a smile.

He and the Elf take a step deeper into the gallery, heads swivelling as they try to take in everything at once. I try to act as Mother always demands, cool and in control, down to the fine hairs at the back of my neck.

But I feel like I'm going to be sick.

"Donovan," I say, trying to muster up literally any thought that isn't a scream.

"I thought you'd be more excited to see me," he confesses, producing an invitation. "I didn't realise your work was so..."

Here it is. At long last, the other shoe is dropping. He's going to repeat exactly what Mother did months ago. He's not going to see this place the way I do. He isn't going to understand and he's going to belittle it.

"Evocative," he finally says.

I blink in confusion. What did he say?

"I can't believe it's taken me this long to come to one of your shows," he continues. "I-I know we haven't always gotten on, but my eyes have recently been opened."

"You have a life," I say. "A peerage and all."

"But you are my family. We are your family too."

As he says the words, he takes hold of the Elf's hand and places the other over his stomach. I blink again. Is he trying to tell me he's pregnant?

"You remember the High Elf Clan of Bramblebliss? This is their heir, Haemir, and he is my mate."

I'm going to faint. Is this why Angelica was so furious with him? Because he's having a child out of wedlock with an Elf?

"Recent page, three stars," he jokes, soft burr in his voice. "Though I think they've already forgotten since the binding ceremony was announced."

"Oh, wow." I'm unable to keep the surprise out of my voice. Typical, the High Elves would be quick to announce such a serious ceremony if they're soon to have a new Elfling.

That makes much more sense. This would send Mother into a spiral, especially from her golden child. But the surprise wears off quickly when I remind myself he's not really my family anymore.

"I assume she told you I've been cut off for good then?" I ask.

"Well, about that," he chuckles nervously. "It's sort of the opposite."

"Opposite of what?" Mitch says, materialising next to me.

Another hand wraps around my side, as Clay steps up. I'm surrounded by the smell of sweet pastries and safety. My mates stare down my brother.

"Donovan, this is Clay and Mitch"—I gesture to each of them—"my mates."

I'm not so distracted by his stunned expression to miss the way Donovan and Haemir lean back. The slight is plain as day. My brother and his mate think less of my lads.

"Yes, well." He clears his throat. "As I'm marrying into a royal family, I can't accept our family's title. It falls to you, or we lose it to some distant leech of a cousin. So we need you to come home. You can still be an artist, and Mummy won't control your funds anymore, and—"

"I'm already home." I stop him. "Hallow's Cove is my home."

"But Rowey—" he insists.

"Her name is Roan," Clay states. His voice is a threatening, almost snarl. His anger bristles right beneath the surface.

"You'd really give up your life for this?" He looks around again, like he's trying to scan for faults.

"I'm giving up the life Mother wanted for me," I counter. "My life here is richer than it ever was in London."

"But—"

"No buts." I shrug. "Please enjoy the refreshments and the art. Maybe you'll learn something."

I take hold of my mates and we move around my brother, down the stairs and out the door. A breath of fresh air hits me, and I feel like I can truly relax now. Maybe it's a little early to call it, but I think that was a success. I really did it—we really did it. A fluttering warmth tickles my chest when I think about all the work that went into making this possible.

It's not a fancy show in London with all the papers and media, but this was *my* show. The people here don't need to write reviews for me to see their appreciation. Their smiles and excitement were enough. I'm surrounded by the people who are here because I want them to be, because they want to be a part of my life.

We don't speak as we sneak away to the café. I look back at the lights of the Cove Arts Centre and stop. The windows glow brightly, the shadow of people just visible on the first floor. It almost looks like a picture you'd see on a postcard. Mitch wraps his arm around my shoulder as Clay pulls out the keys to the front door.

The bell jingles like a soft coming home.

When the door is locked up again, Clay swoops in. He picks me up by the waist and swings me around until I'm giggling and begging to be on solid ground. Mitch is behind the counter, bent over and digging for something.

With as much class and authority as a judge, he squirts a huge swirl of whipped cream into his mouth. I dizzily step towards the counter and present my mouth. The harsh sound of the nozzle makes me squint, just in case it goes crazy again, but sweet vanilla cream hits my tongue and I hum at its perfection.

"Animals," Clay mutters, digging out a pie that didn't sell today. He drops it on the counter, along with three forks. "Cream me, Beta."

Mitch snorts, but does as he's told. Three swirls mark our sections of the pie as we dig in. Tangy, sweet blueberry bursts on my tongue as buttery, flaky crusts melts in my mouth.

"The perfect pudding." I smile.

"For the perfect pack," Mitch says.

Clay pulls us together. "Damn fucking straight."

Thank you for reading!

Wolves and Whipped Cream was a delight to write, and I hope it was just as much as a delight for you to read! If you enjoyed this book, please consider leaving a review. It helps indie authors like me get our books in front of more people.

A big shout out to Lyonne and Jen for beta reading and supporting me during the writing process, and to the rest of the Hallow's Cove authors for their support. This has been an amazing project to participate in!

If you'd like to get a signed paperback copy of Wolves and Whipped Cream, check out my shop.

Are you mad there wasn't a DP scene? Sign up to my newsletter to get access to the bonus epilogue with heats, cosplay, and DP!

Want to know about everything happen in my world and see some of the scenes from this book censor free? Check out my patreon.

Love to the Raven's Nest

A big thank you to all my Patreon supporters, with special shout out to:

Sue, Lauren, LogeyB, Emmy, Nicole, Erin, GracieBlue, Tysharina, Heather, Dajana, Shell, Jemmique, Ilana, Aden, lovetostitch, Heather, Ash, Emily S., Alexandria, Bree, hailsunshine, AIM, Kitty, Sarah, Christine, Tracy, Melanie, Kbucky, Faye, Andi, Biscuitquick, Kels

Hallow's Cove

Also by Ash Raven

Check out the Sins of The Flesh series.

The Librarian of Souls
The Pirate Queen of Ruin
The Widow of Fortune
The Kingpin of Magic

Check out the First Date Abductions series.

Jumping the Shark: Matched with the Space Shark

Check out the Benetti Werewolf Mafia series.

Claimed by the Werewolf Boss

About the Author

ASH RAVEN IS AN indie author who specialises in spicy monster and alien romances that focus on plus-size and LGBTQ+ leads who get the love of a lifetime. They strive to write stories that are inclusive and real, with a touch of magic and a boat load of spice. When they are not writing, they are cuddling with their two orange cats and drinking oat mochas through a straw. They have been living their own insta-love romance in London, UK since 2015.

Want to know more? You can find Ash on most social media as @authorashraven or subscribe to their newsletter for exclusive updates, art prints, and cat pictures.